J. T. EDSON'S
FLOATING OUTFIT

The toughest bunch of Rebels that ever lost a war, they fought for the South, and then for Texas, as the legendary Floating Outfit of "Ole Devil" Hardin's O.D. Connected ranch.

MARK COUNTER was the best dressed man in the West: always dressed fit-to-kill. BELLE BOYD was as deadly as she was beautiful, with a "Manhattan" model Colt tucked under her long skirts. THE YSABEL KID was Comanche fast and Texas tough. And the most famous of them all was DUSTY FOG, the ex-cavalryman known as the Rio Hondo Gun Wizard.

J. T. Edson has captured all the excitement and adventure of the raw frontier in this magnificent Western Series. Turn the page for a complete list of Floating Outfit titles.

J. T. EDSON'S
FLOATING OUTFIT
WESTERN ADVENTURES

J. T. EDSON'S
CIVIL WAR SERIES

J.T. Edson

TRAIL BOSS

CHARTER BOOKS, NEW YORK

Originally published in Great Britain
by Brown Watson, Ltd.

This Charter book contains the complete
text of the original edition.
It has been completely reset in a typeface
designed for easy reading, and was printed
from new film.

TRAIL BOSS

A Charter Book / published by arrangement with
Transworld Publishers, Ltd.

PRINTING HISTORY
Corgi edition published 1968
Berkley edition / November 1980
Charter edition / October 1987

ISBN: 0-441-82097-2

Charter Books are published by The Berkley Publishing Group,
200 Madison Avenue, New York, New York 10016.
The name "CHARTER" and the "C" logo
are trademarks belonging to Charter Communications, Inc.

PRINTED IN THE UNITED STATES OF AMERICA

10   9   8   7   6   5   4   3   2   1

For Dorothy,
who has put up with me for years.

CHAPTER ONE

Bring Back A Trail Boss

"Bring back a trail boss."

The words beat a tattoo in Thora Holland's brain, beat it in rhythm to the hooves of the chuckwagon's team as she sat on the hard, uncomfortable seat.

A trail boss was the thing the Rocking H wanted, just one man.

But not any man would do.

A trail boss was a man amongst men; only a trail boss could cope with the many problems of trailing three thousand head of half-wild Texas longhorns north to the shipping pens at Dodge City. To do that he had to be tough, aggressive, intelligent and quick to deal with any emergency.

On any drive he needed all those qualifications; he needed them even moreso on this drive. This Rocking H herd would have to be taken all the long miles north, up through the Texas Panhandle, over the North Brazos, the Red, the Cimmaron, the Canadian and other smaller rivers. It would have trouble with these as the season was early and the winter snows would still be raising the river level. These problems were enough, but there were others, not the least of which was Jethro Kliddoe and his bunch of reb-hating Kansas border ruffians.

Thora shivered at the thought of Kliddoe; the name struck a chill into her. Kliddoe and his men would be something more than the ordinary hazard for the trail boss to handle.

The trail boss was needed to handle the drive; but where could an Eastern woman find such a man?

Thora thought of all she had heard about the duties of a trail boss and the creed by which he was judged. Ben Holland, her husband, had told her of it often. How a trail boss left Texas with a herd, fed beef to the hands all the way north, lost a few head on the trail and still reached the shipping pens with more than he started out.

This consisted of a three-foot-long iron rod with a handle at one end and a reversed facsimile of the outfit's chosen brand at the other.

Ben Holland knew this creed well enough. Before his accident his name as a trail boss was assured. Then bushwhack lead left him a cripple in a wheelchair. With Ben on his feet there would have been none of this worry about getting a crew to go north with the trail herd.

It had been in Dodge that Ben was shot. The ambush had been well laid, but the bushwhacker showed caution. The charge from his ten-gauge shotgun crippled instead of killed.

That was some trip, Ben's last drive north the previous spring. In Dodge he ran foul of a pious assistant deputy called Wyatt Earp. Earp was about to pistol-whip a drunken young Texas cowhand, but Ben intervened. There was no trouble. Earp declined to fight a sober man of his own size, but he made muttered threats.

After Ben was shot Bat Masterson investigated, but found nothing to help him in his search. He was a friend of both Earp and Ben Holland and checked on Earp's whereabouts to prove one thing or the other. Earp had left Dodge the morning after the clash. There was nothing to connect him with the attempted murder.

Masterson tried to find who did the shooting. Ben was well liked by folks in Dodge and had no enemies. Only one significant point came out of the business. After his return to Dodge, while Ben was being taken back to Texas in the wagon, Earp passed word that the Rocking H must not use the Dodge City pens again.

That was just one more problem the trail boss must handle if he took the herd to Dodge. Just one more trial in the arduous task ahead of the Rocking H trail boss.

It was a true saying, Thora thought, that it never rained but it poured. With all this against them, they get trouble nearer at hand. Ben's crew had made an early roundup and had collected their trail herd; they had only completed road branding it the day before. Then their neighbor, Thad Toon of the Double T, an old enemy of the Rocking H, made his move. Toon had begun his roundup after Ben's crew started theirs and was trying to catch up on their lead. He knew that by fair means he could not get his herd on the trail first, so he made his move. Hiring a fast-gun killer, he set up camp in the town of Granite and passed word that any man hiring to Rocking H would be buying grief.

With Ben off his feet, and without a leader, it had worked. No man had offered to hire.

That was the sort of problem Ben could have handled easily had he been on his feet. Now it lay to Thora to do the best she could. It had taken much argument and pleading before Ben would allow her to go into Granite and try to hire men. At last Ben had given in; and so she sat here this cold morning by the side of Salt Ballew, the cook, headed for Granite.

She made a pretty picture sitting on the hard seat of the Rocking H chuck wagon. A tall, mature woman with golden blonde hair hanging from under the brim of her Stetson hat. Not even the heavy coat she wore could hide the rich fullness of her body, the gentle swell of her breasts, the slimness of her waist and the strong, firm curves of her hips and legs.

Turning, she looked at the man by her side. He was as typical a product of the Texas range as she obviously wasn't. Salt Ballew was six-foot-odd of oak-brown sinew and whang leather. His range clothes were clean, well worn, and around his waist was a gunbelt supporting his old Dance Bros. percussion revolver.

Salt was handling the team with the same relaxed competence that showed in everything he did. He was just as much at ease, and as capable, whether he was cooking up a meal out in the open in a half gale, driving a two-mule team, or sitting round the fire in the cook-shack and spinning tall tales about the Mexican War. He looked like what he was, an old-time range cook, master of his trade, hard, tough, ornery, and respected by the crew for it.

"Will we get the men, Salt?" she asked.

"Men's there, Miz Thora," he replied, his lazy drawl a contrast from her Eastern accents. "Want work, and r'aring to go. But they wants a leader, which same we can't give them. Sort of men we wants won't just foller any man."

"I'm going."

"Sort of men we wants won't foller no woman. We needs the best happen we have to face Earp and his friends."

Thora thought this over for a moment. "A lawman can't stop us from taking the herd into Dodge, just for a grudge, can he?"

"Law don't come into it. There ain't much law for Texas men north of the Indian Nations. Anyways, Earp ain't the law. He's just one of the extra hands they takes on while the trail driving season's on. But he surely wants to make hisself a name as a lawman. There's plenty of ripe pickings for a man who can. So he's making this play against the Rocking H. If we don't take the herd, he's made his play. The Rocking H has a name and the man who can scare off Ben Holland's somebody. If we go up we've called his bluff and he'll have to show down."

Thora had long since learned to listen when Salt Ballew gave out his wisdom, for it was mostly right. He had experience in the West and she had need of that experience now.

"How about Thad Toon?" she inquired; she had only met him once.

"Thad ain't bad. Jest a mite ornery 'n' none too bright. He ain't been overfond of Ben since we built up our herd with all that unbranded stock, after the war. Ben even offered to throw in with Thad to cut out all the range, but Thad got mean and wouldn't. Ole Thad's been waiting all this time to get evens."

"With Ben in the wheelchair he should stop us," Thora agreed, bitterly. "I'm going to see the sheriff——"

"Thad don't want to stop us going. Jest wants to get off afore we do."

"Is that important?"

"Surely is. First off gets the pick of the grazing all the way north. Gets the best prices in Dodge. There's a lot to being first herd into Dodge."

Thora knew something of the loyalty of the cowhands to the brand and knew that every ranch crew wanted their own spread to have the best possible record and reputation in matters concerning the cattle business. However, the Rocking H couldn't spare the men, and the trail drive crew would be strangers who did not have that same loyalty.

"Can't the law help," she asked, "with that gunman in town threatening any man who takes on for us?"

Salt sent a spurt of tobacco at a small rock before replying. "Ain't much the town marshal can do. Anyways, the men'd hire, happen we had a trail boss. It'd take more than a hired gun to stop hands going up trail."

Thora sat back. She hardly noticed they were almost into the town of Granite. There was so much she didn't know about the cattle business and so much she was going to have to know if she was to get that herd to market. That was work for a man and a highly skilled man at that—not for a young woman who'd only been in the West for three years.

Thora was aware of her limitations. She had never been west until meeting Ben in Chicago. They married after a short courtship and he had brought her to his ranch in Texas. At the ranch she was accepted as the boss's wife. The hands treated her with respect, yet they didn't accept her as one of them. She was a Yankee knowing nothing of cattle business.

That hadn't mattered with Ben on his feet, where all she needed to do was run the house. Now she was to take her husband's place and learn the cattle business under the most difficult of conditions.

"Excuse me, ma'am," a voice, a soft, pleasing Texas drawl, came from her side of the wagon.

Thora and Salt both looked at the speaker, but they saw him with different eyes.

Thora saw a small, insignificant man riding a big paint horse. She noted a black, low-crowned, wide-brimmed hat on dusty blond hair. The face was handsome, young looking and friendly. Around his neck was a long, tight-rolled blue bandanna, the ends falling over his faded blue shirt almost to the waistband of his Levi's. The cuffs of his Levi's were turned back and hung outside his high-heeled riding boots with their big spurs. She hardly noted the gunbelt and doubted if he could use the guns in the holsters.

Salt was looking at the same man, but he was looking with rangewise eyes that knew cowhands. He saw a face which was young, yet old in wisdom; cool grey eyes which looked right through a man; a mouth which had grin quirks at the corners, yet was firm. The jaw below showed strength of character.

The cook's eyes went to the hat—an expensive J.B. Stetson; that hat had cost plenty. Next he looked at the boots and the double-girthed Texas saddle; they were expensive and the maker of them——

Salt's eyes went to the gunbelt and a whistle of surprise came from his lips. That gunbelt had been made by the same man who made the saddle and boots, a man famous for his leatherwork. But that buscadero gunbelt told a man things. Ole Joe Gaylin of El Paso had made the belt. He would sell his boots and saddles to anyone who had his prices, but they were high. His gunbelts were something again. Joe Gaylin wouldn't sell them to just anyone; he chose the men who wore his gunbelts. To wear a Joe Gaylin gunbelt, a man had to be somebody. That belt, with the matched bone-handled Colt 1860 Army revolvers, butt forward for a cross draw, had been made by Joe Gaylin.

The horse told Salt more about the small man. It was seventeen hands of paint stallion, not the horse for a beginner to try out on. A man had to be better than average happen he wanted to stay on top of that horse and not end picking its shoes out of his teeth.

So where Thora saw a quiet, insignificant young man

riding a big paint horse, Salt saw a tophand whose twin, bone-handled guns, rope, and Winchester 66 carbine had all seen expert use.

"I hear you're hiring a trail crew, ma'am," the small man went on.

"We are!" Thora managed to hide her disappointment that this small man should be the first to offer his services. He didn't look the sort who could face hired killers.

"There are three of us." The small man indicated the others.

Salt and Thora turned and looked. They had been so interested in this small man that they hadn't heard the other two riding on the other side. Thora nodded in approval; these were the sort of men she wanted.

Both were tall, one six foot, the other three inches more than that. The latter took Thora's eyes right away; he would catch the eye in any company. Thora thought he was the most handsome man she had ever seen. His hat was a costly, low-crowned, wide-brimmed, white J.B. Stetson, set back on his curly, golden blond hair. His clothes were expensive and he was a cowhand fashion plate from the silver concha-decorated hatband, through his multihued silk bandanna, expensive doeskin shirt, new Levi's, and fancy-stitched boots. Around his slim waist was a hand-carved gunbelt with a matched brace of Colt 1860 revolvers, the butts flaring to his hands.

Salt studied the dandy rig of the cowhand, noted the width of the shoulders, the slim waist. The fancy dress of the big man might have turned Salt off, but that too was a Gaylin gunbelt. The man rode a blood bay stallion as big as the paint, rode it easily, being a light rider in spite of his size.

To Salt it all read clear; here was another tophand.

The third man was lean and lithe, but he looked as tough as whipcord. He appeared to be about sixteen years old, his face young, almost babyishly young. Yet the red hazel eyes were not young, they were old, cold, and dangerous. Salt saw more than just a young, black-dressed boy on a magnificent white stallion.

The young man wore all black, from his hat to his boots. Even his gunbelt was black; only the butt-forward, walnut grips of the old Dragoon Colt at his right side and the ivory hilt of the bowie knife at his left relieved the blackness.

Salt felt uneasy as he looked this young man over. He wore a cowhand's rig all right, but Salt felt that he had learned the cattle business along the Rio Grande on dark nights.

The old Dragoon Colt told a man things, happen he knew what to look for. In the year of 1870, Colt's 1860 Army revolver had been on the market for long enough and enough of them had been produced to have seen most of the old four-pound Dragoon guns put aside as out of date. For a man to be wearing one these days usually meant that he was behind the times and was looked down on for it. Somehow, Salt got the idea that this didn't apply to the black-dressed boy. In a tight fix it would be to the hilt of the bowie knife his hand would fly to first, the revolver second.

They were a pair to draw to, those riders—tophands both and fighting men from soda to hock, Salt thought. Yet strangely the third man, the small, insignificant Texas man at the other side, wasn't out of place in such company.

"I think we could use you," Thora replied, having decided that, if these three took on, others might be willing to join. "Have you ever been to Dodge City?"

"No, ma'am," the tallest of the trio replied. "Hays once, Newton once."

"Happen we're lucky," the black-dressed boy went on. "We'll find where she lies."

Salt craned his neck, trying to discover what brands the horses wore, particularly the big paint, but he couldn't see it. He had a vague, uneasy feeling that he could name these three young men. If his guess was right, the Rocking H were having more luck than they could rightly expect.

The cook glanced ahead to where three men had left one of the saloons and were looking toward the wagon. In a few minutes, he thought, a man would know just how good his guessing was.

Thora caught Salt's eye and looked ahead; she felt a sudden panic as she watched the three men stepping from the sidewalk and moving out until they blocked the trail. Two of them she knew; the man at the right, big, well dressed, wide shouldered, hand resting on the butt of his Colt, was Thad Toon, owner of the TT.

The man at the left of the trail was shorter, stocky, and hard-looking. That was Joel Hendley, Toon's foreman, a tough man and handy with his old Navy Colt.

It was the rider in the center of the trail who caught and held Thora's attention. He was a tall man, dressed in the style Wild Bill Hickok affected in town. His hat was a low-crowned J. B. Stetson, his black coat, frilly-bosomed shirt, and tight-legged white trousers were all well tailored, his store shoes shining. Around his waist was a silk sash and a pearl-handled Remington revolver was thrust into it. It was the face that held her eyes. A face that was cold, expressionless, with eyes as hard and unfeeling as a snake.

Thora had seen gunfighters before; she knew without being told that this was the killer who had been hired to prevent men taking on to drive for Rocking H. She looked at the three young men by her side; they were lounging in their saddles, looking over the Double T riders without any knowledge of their danger. She could not let them be shot down by this hired killer.

Toon stood silent for a few moments, then looked Thora and Salt over. Finally he spoke to the three young Texas cowhands.

"That's the Rocking H wagon you're riding with," he said softly.

"Now me, I thought it was the President's carriage.

Was all set to take off my hat and cheer," the dark boy on the white horse replied.

Toon looked up sharply, taking in every detail of the mocking-voiced youngster. "I put the Injun sign on that spread, sonny. Likewise passed the word that nobody hires to them."

"Waal, now." The tallest of the trio's voice was a deep, southern drawl. "That's for the lady to say, her being from the Rocking H and all."

"Funny bunch, huh?" Hendley growled before his boss could speak. "We got us a real bunch of funny men here, ain't we, Ed?"

"Yeah." The hired killer's voice was harsh and menacing. "We sure have Joel. Likely they'll laugh themselves to death."

The small man had been watching all this. He spoke, his voice mild. "You mean you're asking us not to hire to Rocking H?"

"The boss here don't ask cowhands nothing," the hired killer answered. "He's *telling* you—and I'm here to see you does as he tells you."

"Mean he's ordering us?" There was a deceptive mildness in the big cowhand's tones.

"Just that."

"Well now, I never was much of a hand at taking orders. Fact being that ole General Bushrod Sheldon always said I was the worse order-taking soldier in his command."

"That means you aims to take on agin the boss's orders?" asked the killer tensing slightly, his hand lifting.

Toon flashed a glance at the hired gun. He didn't want these three young men shooting if he could help it. Like Salt, he could tell good hands when he saw them and he had need of good hands for his own trail drive.

"This here's Ed Wren," he said warningly.

If he expected any sign of fear, or any other emotion, at the mention of the name, he was sadly disappointed. Not one of the three gave any sign of ever having heard of the man called Ed Wren.

The three young Texans still remained lounging in their saddles; they studied the hired killer. Then the dark young man replied, his tones mocking and sardonic.

"Waal now, seeing's how we're all so cosy and being real formal like, allow me to present us. I'm Loncey Dalton Ysabel. This here gent on the blood bay's Mark Counter." He paused for a couple of seconds, to let the names sink in, noting the worry lines which were forming on two of the faces. "This here," he waved a hand toward the small rider. "Ain't nobody much at all. Happen you never even heard of him." He paused, then:

"His name is Dusty Fog!"

CHAPTER TWO

The Immortal Words of Colonel Sam

"Dusty Fog!" In all her life Thora had never heard four voices put so much different expression into just two small words. There was wild elation in old Salt's whoop as his suspicions were confirmed. Toon's startled croak showed his worry, and there was fear and uneasiness in Hendley's tones. Only the hired killer's voice held a sneering disbelief.

To Thora alone the name meant very little, at the moment. She tried to remember what she had heard about a man called Dusty Fog.

"Him!" The hired killer jerked a contemptuous thumb at the small Texan. "A short runt like that, Dusty Fog! Who the hell are you——?"

"Mister!" There was a flat and sudden menace in the small man's soft-drawled words. "Leave us remember the immortal words of Colonel Sam Colt:

> *'Be not afraid of any man,*
> *No matter what your size.*
> *When danger threatens, call on me,*
> *And I will equalize.' "*

Ed Wren scowled; he wasn't used to prospective victims spouting poetry at him. "Meaning?" he hissed.

"When ole Colonel Sam brought out his first six-gun, back to Paterson in the old days, he made you and me both the same height."

Thad Toon licked his lips nervously. "Now easy, Dusty." He, for one, didn't doubt who this small, soft-spoken young man was. "We ain't after no fussings with

12

you three; our fight's with the Rocking H."

Thora's mouth opened to claim the three men were hired to her; she closed it again when she realized that she had not told the three cowhands whether they were hired or not. She wanted to say something and try to avert the trouble which plainly was coming. Before she could do so, Dusty Fog took the matter out of her hands.

Without taking his eyes from the hired killer, Dusty reached back and unstrapped the bedroll from behind his saddle. Holding it one-handed, he said, "Excuse me, ma'am. Cookie, throw her in the wagon."

Salt rose and reached over in front of Thora to take the bedroll, a broad grin of pure delight on his seamed face. He took the bedroll and swung it back into the wagon with a delighted, "Sure thing, Cap'n Fog, suh, sure thing."

Thora got the feeling that she had somehow missed something, a sign of some kind. There was a stiffness in the three men standing before her, a tension in the air that hadn't been there before. She alone didn't know the full significance of Dusty's action. The others knew it well, too well. They knew that when a cowhand threw his bedroll into the wagon he became part of the outfit, and any trouble the spread got into was his trouble. It meant that he was fully committed to the brand; their fun his fun; their fight now his fight.

Toon and his two men knew it and they knew that they would have to fuss with Dusty Fog, Mark Counter and the Ysabel Kid if they fussed with the Rocking H.

Mark and the Kid had handed their bedrolls up to the cook, just to show where their feelings in the matter lay. The action had not gone unnoticed by Thad Toon; he was even more disturbed by the action, for he knew much of those three young men.

Dusty watched the hired killer all the time and spoke to Salt. "Start the wagon, Cookie."

Salt reached for the ribbons, his eyes watching the Double T men ahead. "They's in the way, Cap'n."

"Happen they'll move."

Thora had a sudden feeling that she should say or do something to stop this small man getting hurt. Before she could make up her mind to say something, Salt had twitched the reins gently against the sides of his mules. The wagon started to move, flanked by the three cowhands.

Toon and Hendley stood still for a moment. Then they moved aside, having decided that war was off for this day. Ed Wren stood firm, his hand lifting, for he was paid to fight. He was a paid killer and had his reputation to consider. To back out of a fight would mean that his future employers would remember and not pay so well. He thought of this and made his move.

It was a good move in any company, any but the present.

Thora saw the dandy-dressed killer's hand lash across his body to the butt of his gun. The move was fast. Faster, to her terrified eyes, than any other she had seen.

The crash of a shot made her start up, the concussion of the explosion jarring at her nerves and the acrid smell of burnt powder coming to her nostrils. Ed Wren pitched to one side, blood running from the side of his head. His gun fell from his hand, unfired, and landed in the dust of the trail. He crashed down by the side of it an instant later.

Twisting round, Thora looked down at the small Texan. Somehow, Dusty looked taller than any other man here. He sat lounging in the saddle, his left hand holding a smoking revolver. Dusty lifted the gun to his lips and blew smoke from the barrel, then spun it round and holstered it.

The big paint moved forward, passed in front of the wagon and halted in front of Thad Toon. Cold grey eyes looked down at the rancher and a soft voice drawled, "I only creased your hired man, mister. The next time I have to shoot, I'll kill—and it won't only be the hired man I go after."

The Rocking H wagon carried on and Thora leaned over to see what was happening back along the street.

Mark and the Kid stopped their horses and were watching while Dusty spoke to Toon. She turned back to Salt. "Who did they say he was?" she asked.

"Why, Miz Thora, ma'am. That's Cap'n Dusty Fog of the Texas Light Cavalry."

The name didn't mean much to her, she was still confused by all that had happened. "Is he really fast with a gun?"

"Waal now, Miz Thora," Salt scratched his jaw thoughtfully, "I wouldn't go and say he was fast, ma'am. See, take men like Wes Hardin, King Fisher, Bill Longley or Ben Thompson, they're real fast with a gun."

"Well?"

"Ma'am, sides of Cap'n Fog they're only l'arning."

Thora gulped, and sank back in her seat. The men named were the best exponents of gunwork Texas had produced. She wondered what kind of men she had hired.

Salt could have told her something about them, things he had heard in the years since the war.

Dusty Fog might look like a quiet, unassuming young man. He might be passed over unnoticed in a crowd, but not if the crowd were painted for war. At fifteen, he had joined the Texas Light Cavalry in the War Between the States; a year later he had been a captain and for two years had made a name for himself. It was a name that ranked with Turner Ashby and John Singleton Mosby as the supreme raiders of the Confederacy. Where Ashby and Mosby had fought in the more publicized East, Dusty had led his men to harass the Yankee troops in Texas and New Mexico. In doing so he had caused many a Yankee commander to wish that he was dealing with an older and more conventional fighting man.

After the war, Dusty had been selected to go into Mexico and bring back Bushrod Sheldon and his men, who were serving Maximillian. That was where he had teamed up with Mark and the Kid. Since then, they had ridden for Dusty's uncle, Ole Devil Hardin.

Mark Counter could have carved a name for himself in the annals of border gunfighting, had he not chosen to ride with Dusty. He had been a Lieutenant under Sheldon and was said to be the finest all-round fighting man in the West. He was faster than most with his guns, a better than fair shot with a rifle and as a fist-fighter had few equals. He was a tophand and knew cattle if anything better than Dusty did. His father owned the biggest ranch down in the Texas Big Bend country, but Mark preferred to ride with Dusty and the Kid as part of Ole Devil's floating outfit.

The Ysabel Kid was last, but by no means least, of this trio; they tell many tales of the Ysabel Kid down in Mexico. He might look young and innocent, but men who had seen him in a fight knew how far the innocence went. He was good with his old Dragoon gun, the finest exponent of the art of cut-and-slash since James Bowie went to his death at the Alamo. It was with his rifle that he excelled; there was a saying down on the Rio Grande about the Kid and his Winchester 66: "When the Ysabel Kid hits his mark it is ordinary; when he misses it is a miracle."

There was more than just a bone-touch fighting man to the Ysabel Kid; he was acknowledged as a first-rate tracker and reader of sign and as a student of Indian ways. His knowledge of Spanish was only exceeded by his mastery of six Indian tongues.

All in all, although Thora didn't know this, Dusty Fog, Mark Counter and the Ysabel Kid were good friends to have in a fight; they were also real bad enemies.

The three young men rode up alongside the wagon again and not one of them gave so much as a look behind them at Toon and Hendley. Dusty smiled up at her, and he looked young and insignificant again. "Didn't have a chance to tell you before, ma'am, but Uncle Devil sent me along to be trail boss when he heard about Cousin Ben's trouble."

Thora frowned; she was willing to accept Dusty as a hand, but he looked too young to be able to handle the dangerous task of being a trail boss. Then she remembered how fast Ed Wren had grabbed for his gun, and how this small man had beaten him to the shot—also the worried look on Toon's face when he heard who the small man was.

Whatever misgivings Thora might have had, Salt Ballew didn't show any. He greeted Dusty's words with a yell of delight. "Yowee!" he howled. "We don't have us no more worries now, Miz Thora. Men'll come in faster than a Texas blue norther when they hears Cap'n Fog's riding trail boss. We'll certain be plumb belly-deep in pick of the town."

Thora thought this over for a moment; she could not remember her husband ever mentioning anybody called "Devil" and wondered who he was that he should send men to help her out. "Do you know Ben?" she asked more to cover her lack of decision than for any desire of information.

"He's nodding kin," Dusty replied. "Met him one time when he came to the Rio Hondo for the Christmas turkey-shoot."

Thora nodded; she could see how she had not heard much about this relative of her husband. Since coming west she had learned something of the kin system of the South. Nodding kin were distant relations and she wondered why one would take the trouble of helping out the Rocking H.

The town marshal stepped from his office; he had been a witness to all that had happened along the street and seen the shooting. Now the wagon had arrived, he stepped out to have a word with them.

Salt halted the wagon and the three cowhands also stopped, each lounging in the saddle and looking down at the marshal. Looking back, he asked, "He dead?"

"Nope," Mark replied. "All cooks look like that."

"Not Salt. I know he ain't but half dead—and that only from the Stetson down. I meant Ed Wren."

"Just creased," Dusty answered. "You should keep such evildoers out of your town, Frank."

The marshal didn't take any offense at this and turned his attention to Dusty. "I try, I try. So the sooner you three hellers light out the happier I'll be. I can do with you here the same way I can use a hole in the top of my head."

"That'd be what I'd call an improvement," the Kid replied.

Thora started to get to her feet; she knew the marshal was a fair and brave man and expected to see her three hands thrown into jail for the shooting. They didn't seem to be trying to avoid it, with their attitude toward the marshal. "Captain Fog is my trail boss," she put in hotly, then realized she had committed herself now. "We only came to hire hands; after that we'll be going. You know that Thad Toon had that man in town to stop us hiring——"

"Yes, ma'am," the marshal interrupted with a wink at the three cowhands. "I know what Thad's been saying and wondered just when somebody'd take up that fancy-dressed gunslick." He looked along the street to where Toon and Hendley were carrying the gunman toward the doctor's house. "I'll have a few words with Thad. Don't you worry none, Miz Thora, with Dusty here as trail boss you'll get your crew, the town's full of men all looking for work."

"Thank you." Thora saw that her crew was in no danger of being arrested. "I'm sorry it came to shooting."

The marshal grinned. "So's ole Thad I reckon." The grin faded. "You heard that Kliddoe's got a new bunch and working the Dodge City area?"

"We heard." Dusty didn't sound any too worried by the prospect. "I reckon we'll just have to hope and pray we slip by him."

The marshal could see that trio of hell-twisters doing any praying over a thing like that. He lifted his hand in a cheery salute. Then he turned to head down the street, to tell Thad Toon something to his advantage.

Granite City wasn't much different from a hundred other such towns in the West. The business section, comprising stores, saloons and the jail, shared the main drag with the Granite Hotel—the finest, in fact the only, hotel in town. Outside this imposing building Salt halted his team.

Mark helped Thora down from the wagon and then the three young men attended to their horses. They returned to join her on the porch and Dusty pulled a chair up for her, then sat on the rail with his back to the street. For a moment Thora thought that he was showing a lamentable lack of precaution, presenting his back to anyone coming toward them. Then she saw that Mark and the Kid were lounging on either side of her and all were in a position to cover the others' blind spots. She saw that Salt was down at the store getting last-minute purchases for the drive.

Dusty asked for permission to smoke and then rolled three smokes one after the other. She watched his hands at work and realized that he was using his right hand now, not his left. She didn't know it but Dusty was completely ambidextrous. He had trained himself to be that way since his early school days. It had been part of his defense against his lack of inches, a defense which had driven him to become the chain-lightning gun-handler that he was.

"Do you know what they say about the herd?" she asked.

"Sure, they're offering five-to-one it doesn't get through, back in Fort Worth." Dusty replied. "I've ten dollars on it."

"There's a lot against our getting through."

"Man'd say you called that right. I heard about Cousin Ben getting gunned in Dodge. Word has it that a friend of Earp, skin hunter called Shag Moxel, boasted he'd done it."

"Yeah," the Kid put in. "Happen we'll know the truth when we get up there."

"You mean that, knowing about Earp's threat, you're willing to go to Dodge?"

"Sure." It was Mark who answered her startled query. "Earp doesn't mean a thing. And don't tell me about him arresting Ben Thompson in Ellsworth: I was there and know what happened. Earp's just a loudmouth who likes a badge to hide behind. He's not even a regular lawman in Dodge, just one of the extra hands they take on in the trail season."

"Mark's right!" Dusty agreed. "Earp talks big but he's not big inside, unless he has the backing. Kliddoe scares me more than Earp, and he doesn't scare me all that much."

Thora licked her lips. Kliddoe was one man she didn't want to talk about. "What will you do now?"

"Hire us some men, unless you have enough." Dusty looked along the street as he spoke. "Who was that *hombre* we had words with back there?"

"Thad Toon, owner of the Double T. He's our neighbor and wants to get his herd moved out first."

"Does, huh?" Dusty's smile made him look even younger. "He won't get his wanting."

Thora felt a momentary misgiving at taking on this young man: he would never be able to handle the crew. However, Salt approved of having Dusty Fog as trail boss and Ben had told her to take the cook's advice on such things. She knew that Salt would never lead her wrong on a matter as important as this.

"How many men will we need? The herd is about three thousand head."

"How many of your own men are you sending?"

"Salt, his assistant," Thora answered, "and myself."

Three faces looked at hers; it was the first and last time she ever saw them show any surprise. "You, ma'am?" The Ysabel Kid sounded as if he didn't believe his ears.

"A trail drive's no place for a woman, ma'am." Mark took it up. "It's not even a fit place for a man, happen he's got any sense at all."

Dusty didn't speak but watched the young woman's face as she answered them. "I'm the only one who can be spared. We can't do without Salt and his assistant, but we have to. Ben doesn't want me to go, but I can be pretty persuasive when I have to. He's come round to my way of thinking by now. Besides"—her face was flushed—"I have a reason for wanting to go along, a reason that I haven't told Ben. I know a surgeon in the East who may be able to help Ben. I've made arrangements to meet him in Dodge and bring him home to the Rocking H."

"We could bring him for you, ma'am," Mark suggested.

She shook her head. "Doctor Burglin wouldn't come with you. He's rather eccentric and thinks that cowboys aren't to be trusted. He won't come unless I go and fetch him myself."

"All right, ma'am—if that's your reason, you come with us," Dusty drawled.

Thora had two other reasons, but she didn't tell them to these three young men; either one would have turned them off, she thought. She wanted to know more about what they were going to do now. "How many men will you need?"

"About another eighteen or so," Dusty replied. He studied the woman's face for a moment, seeming to be uncomfortable about something. "There's one thing I want understood, ma'am. And I want it understood right from the start. Uncle Devil always taught me one thing, in everything from a Cavalry regiment to a trail drive there can't be but one boss. There can't be two."

"Well?"

"You can come along with us, but I want it understood that either you or I handle the chore of trail boss. If I am, it's my duty to hire, work and fire every man we take on. If you come, you're classed as a hand, the same as the rest. You take my orders."

The two looked at each other for a time. Then she drew herself up proudly. "Captain Fog, my father was a regular officer in the Army and I spent most of my early life in army posts. I learned the same rule as you. If you are the trail boss, I will take your orders."

Grins flickered on three tanned faces. Mark held out a hand the size of a ham. "You'll do, ma'am."

"Reckon you will," Dusty agreed. "Now we'll get the trail crew rounded up. We've got a whole heap of miles to cover, ma'am, and 'Captain' sounds real formal. I'm Dusty, this is Mark and Lon."

"And I'm Thora to my friends." She felt warmer toward the three men now.

"Mark, you 'n' Lon head down to the shanties and roust out a Negro for nighthawk. Pass the word as you go along."

The two men stepped forward obediently and Dusty moved so that he had his back to the wall. He took a chair and sat in it, leaning against the wall.

"How will you get the eighteen men we need?" asked Thora.

"Hire them."

"But do you know that many men in town?"

"Likely know some. We'll get all we want."

Thora sat back; she wondered how Dusty would set about hiring strangers for a difficult business like trail driving. She didn't want him to think she doubted him, so she changed the subject. "How long have you three been together?"

"Since just after the war. We teamed up in Mexico and, when we came north, decided to stick together. Uncle Devil took us on as a floating outfit and we've been riding for him since then."

"Floating outfit?" She looked puzzled. "We don't have one. What do you do?"

"Work round the spread until winter, then head out for the back country. There's five of us and a cook, riding greasy sack most of the time."

"Greasy sack?"

"Sure, we take our food along in sacks on a mule, instead of with a wagon. Call it trailing a long-eared chuck wagon down our way."

Thora relapsed into silence and watched Mark and the Kid entering a saloon. They soon came out and Thora went on talking. "Lon, the Kid, is he as dangerous as he looks?"

"Worse!" There was a smile flickering on Dusty's lips. "He's the only man who scares me."

"Is he—er—is——" She floundered to a stop, not knowing how to carry on or frame her next question.

"Is he white?" The smile had gone and the voice was cold. "He's white clear through, ma'am. His paw was Irish-Kentucky; his mother Creole-Comanche—but he's the whitest man I know, ma'am."

"I didn't mean to insult your friend!" That one word, "ma'am" had been a warning to her. She was coming to dangerous ground. "I haven't been west long enough to have any prejudice against mixed blood. My mother was French and my father Scottish. That is a mixture, too."

"Sure, Thora." The drawl was back, soft and easy again. "We'll soon be getting our crew."

Thora saw that Mark and the Kid were headed toward the shanties where the colored workers of the town lived. She also saw that several cowhands were walking along the street toward the hotel. The men came along; they didn't stop or say anything to Dusty, just walked past and then turned and went back toward the saloon once more.

Then she saw a tall, dark man coming along the street toward the hotel. He wore a low-crowned black Stetson and his clothes were old, untidy, yet his boots were new looking. His face was lean, dark and dangerous looking. He ambled along in a slouching stride, his eyes all the time flickering round and his hands brushing the Remington revolver at his left side and the bowie knife at his right.

She felt a sudden fear; the man looked cold and dangerous, like the pictures she had seen of Quantrel raiders. He must be an outlaw the way he acted, probably a killer. To her horror, Dusty lifted his hand in greeting.

"Howdy, Kiowa!" he said, "You riding?"

CHAPTER THREE

On Choosing Hands

The dark man halted at Dusty's words and glanced at the girl before he replied, "Nope!"

"Need a point man or scout—along of Mark, or ahead with the Kid. You take that?"

"Yep!"

"You heard the word about this herd?"

"Yep!"

Thora had been watching the dark face, which showed no expression at all that she could read. She wondered why Dusty had picked this dark, dangerous-looking man from the crowd. Of course Dusty knew him, but that meant little to her. If she had been hiring, she would have taken someone more presentable.

"Wagon's down there by the store. Throw your bedroll in and come back here." Dusty jerked his thumb in the direction of the Rocking H wagon as he spoke. "I want to light out as soon as we've got the rest of the crew. Who all's in town?"

"Billy Jack, Red Tolliver, Basin Jones and a few more you'll likely know. Want for me to herd them in, happen I see 'em?"

"Be right obliged." Dusty was getting amusement in watching the obvious disapproval on Thora's face.

Kiowa slouched off to collect his horse, moving like a buck Apache on the warpath. Two clean, neatly dressed young cowhands came by; both looked hard at Dusty. For a moment Thora thought they were going to ask Dusty for work, but they passed on. She felt disappointed; they were the sort of men she would have hired, not that dark man.

A tall, gangling man was coming along the street now; she noticed him only because of the tired, miserable and careworn look on his face. She wondered if he had just had very bad news, for every line of him gave that impression.

Once more Dusty raised a hand in greeting. "Howdy, Billy Jack," he said. "You riding?"

The gangling man halted and hitched up his gunbelt as if the low-tied brace of Colt 1860 Army revolvers were a burden to him. He looked even more miserable at the thought of work being forced on him. "You say so, Cap'n."

"Point man along of Mark most of the time. You know this is the Rocking H herd, and what they're saying about it?"

"Nigh on skeers me to death," Billy Jack answered dolefully, his prominent Adam's Apple jumping up and down. "Where at's the wagon?"

"Down there by the store. Kiowa's trailing with us."

"That makes my day." Billy Jack turned and slouched about, still looking the picture of dejection.

"Do you know him?" Thora asked. Dusty nodded. "Then is he always like that?" she went on.

"This is one of his good days," Dusty replied. "You should have seen him the day General Robert E. Lee commended him for bravery in the field."

"Him?" Thora gasped, her surprise making her lose her grammar for a moment.

"Yes'm. Billy Jack was the best top sergeant I ever had."

Thora stirred uneasily in her chair. Dusty watched her out of the corner of his eye and guessed what she was thinking. Had he planned it this way, it couldn't have happened better, for she disapproved of his first two choices. Yet she didn't speak; if she took this she would take any orders he gave. This was why he didn't explain his reasons for picking them.

Thora watched a handsome, tall young man coming toward them. He wore the dress of a cowhand dandy and belted a low-tied, pearl-handled Army Colt. After passing the first two over, she doubted if Dusty would take this man. However, he raised his hand. "Howdy, friend! You riding?"

The man halted. He raised his hat to Thora, then shook his head. "Take on, if you'll have me."

"Point's all filled, but we'll take you."

"*Gracias*. The name's Dude."

"Wagon's by the store, Dude. Throw your roll in."

Thora watched Dude walk away and her frown deepened; it was plain to her that Dusty didn't know the man, yet had hired him. She shook her head, it was all beyond her. The next two men Dusty hired were both well-dressed youngsters, and they also were strangers to him. Why he took them and passed over a couple who looked, to her eyes, like them, she couldn't tell. Dusty's next choice was an untidy-looking man who was also a stranger to Dusty. He came after two who might have been his brothers had passed by and been ignored.

There were seventeen men hired when a thin, freckled youngster riding a sorry-looking paint came up. He halted the paint and asked. "You looking for a wrangler, Cap'n?"

Dusty looked the youngster over; he was wearing cast-off clothing that had seen better days. Tucked in his belt was a worn old model Navy Colt; worn though it was, the weapon was clean and cared for. "Sure. You reckon you can handle it?"

"Sure I can," the boy sounded eager. "I been wrangler on a couple of spreads. Was going to say on a couple of drives, but I wouldn't lie to you, Cap'n."

Dusty bent forward to hide his smile, then jerked a thumb to the wagon. "Your folks say you can go, you head down for the wagon and throw your gear in."

The boy shook his head. "Ain't got no folks. Cap'n. Comanches got them when I was a button."

"But how have you lived since then?" Thora gasped, not having run across an Indian-orphaned waif before.

"Folks took care of me 'til I was old enough to fend

for myself. Then I took out and worked for a cattle spread. Got me a hoss and lit out to see some of the range."

"You eat today, boy?" Dusty inquired, and the boy shook his head. "Best get a meal then, afore we head for the spread; you'll likely be needing one——" He stopped, the boy looked embarrassed and hung his head. Dusty pulled a couple of dollars from his pocket and said, "Here, it's a spread rule that we always pay the wrangler some in advance, happen we get a good one."

The boy took the money eagerly. He was very hungry, but didn't want to let his hero know how near the blanket he was. He turned his horse, muttering his thanks, and rode off toward the livery barn. There, before he went to get himself a much-needed meal, he bought the horse the first grain feed it had had in many days.

Thora shook her head: there were many facets to this small man's character that she didn't know of. "Did you hire that boy out of pity?"

"Nope, I reckon he'll make a hand. He'll handle the remuda all right and comes Dodge he'll have filled out plenty on regular food. Next time he goes north he'll be riding as a hand and, maybe in time, he'll be riding trail boss." Dusty saw a familiar face and greeted another old friend. "Howdy, Red, I'd about given you up. You riding?"

Thora watched the final man walking toward the wagon. The men were all standing round it, some helping Salt to load the supplies. Even from the hotel, Thora could see the delight on her cook's face and knew Salt was satisfied with the men.

"That's eighteen," she remarked. "All we need."

"Sure, now what's worrying you about the men?"

She turned a startled face to him and then laughed. "You knew all along I didn't understand how you picked the men. I still don't. Every time I thought I had your system worked out, you spoiled it."

"There's only one system when you're hiring a man. Look at his boots, then at his hat, then at his hands,"

Dusty replied. "A good hand always buys the best boots and hat he can, no matter what the rest of his rig is like. The two who followed Kiowa along. I reckon you'd have hired them. I didn't; they were nothing but milk-cow riders. Sure they'd got good, clean clothes, but their boots were ready-mades. A hand worth hiring buys his boots made to measure; he knows the extra money spent is worth it. Same with his hat; he buys the best J.B. Stetson he can afford. A cheap woolsey might look good, but come a good rain and the brim starts to flop down. That happens when you're riding to head a stampede in a storm, well it doesn't happen more than once. But with a good Stetson you're safe; it'll hold its shape as long as you have it. You can't wear it out; it'll happen take on some weight with age and get so's you can smell it across a wide room, but it'll never lose its shape."

Thora saw Dusty's point. "But what about their hands?"

"A cowhand handles a rope. It burns callouses into his hands. That shows he's handled a rope regular."

Looking down at Dusty's hands, she saw the marks; but there were other callouses on his forefingers. "And the other callouses, on the fingers?"

"They're from a handling a gun."

"I see." She decided to study the boots and hats of the men when they rejoined Dusty. "But about the dark man—Kiowa, I think you called him."

"Kiowa?" Dusty grinned. "I've know him since I was knee-high to a grasshopper. He rode for Uncle Devil's OD Connected until the country started to get too crowded for him."

"How do you mean?"

"Folks started to build another town thirty miles away. He allowed that the Rio Hondo was getting worse crowded than Chicago and pulled out. But there isn't a better hand at the point and I can't think of three better at riding scout. If it comes to Indian savvy there's only one man in this town who licks him."

"Then shouldn't you have hired that one?"

"Didn't have to—it's Lon," Dusty answered.

"Oh!" Thora could see that her trail boss had thought of about everything. "Will we have Indian trouble?"

"Could have. One time you go through the Nations and you're plumb belly-deep in them all the way. Next time, there isn't a feather in sight, 'cepting that can whistle and fly. But one thing I do know. If we get hit by Indians it won't be because they sneaked by Lon and Kiowa."

Mark and the Kid came round the corner of the saloon, followed by eight or so Negroes. Before they came to the porch, Thora had asked another of the questions which had been puzzling her. "But why didn't the men just come up and ask for work, instead of just walking past?"

"Men as good as Kiowa and Billy Jack don't need to ask for work. There were a couple I know went by, tophands both of them, but I didn't want them. So they just walk by. If I want to hire them I ask; if I don't, well nobody's feelings get hurt."

Mark stepped up on to the porch and pointed to the Negroes. "All want to take on as nighthawk," he remarked.

Dusty rose and went to the edge of the porch to look over the eight men, then asked each one what he could do. Seven out of the eight proudly announced their good behavior and sterling Christian ways. The eighth was a tall, lean, grinning man, wearing an old, collarless shirt and a tattered pair of Confederate army trousers.

"Cap'n, sah," he said, pushing back his beat-up old rebel kepi. "I drinks, I smokes, cusses and chouses them lil ole darkie gals bow-legged but I can sho' herd hosses."

"You handle a big remuda at night?"

"You has it, I'll handle it."

"Got a hoss?"

"Got me 'n ole mule that can see in the night like a hoot owl."

"What do we call you?"

The black face split almost across in a grin. "You

calls me what you likes, sah, as long as you calls me for meals good 'n' regular!"

One of the other Negroes snorted; he didn't take kindly to losing a plum chore like this and sought to discredit the fortunate man. "Cap'n, sah. That there Tarbrush, he ain't fittin' company for gawd-fearing folks."

"Well then." Dusty dipped his hand into his pocket again, "I'll tell you what I'll do. Happen we find any of those god-fearing folks where we're going, I'll surely keep him well away from them." Taking out a coin, Dusty tossed it to the man. "Here, either put it in the church box, or buy the rest of the boys a drink."

The seven unfortunate job-seekers turned and ambled off happily, headed for the shanty-town saloon, to drink the gift away. Tarbrush stood and watched them go. He sighed. "Most wish I hadn't been hired now," he remarked as he turned to go for his mule and few belongings.

Salt returned with the rest of the crew and Thora studied each man; she found that Dusty's three pointers in choosing hands were correct. "What now?" she inquired.

"I'll take the boys in for a drink. Then we'll light out for the Rocking H," Dusty replied. He turned his attention to Salt. "How near to ready for rolling are you?"

"Herd's road-branded and ready to go, Cap'n."

"I mean the chuck wagon."

"Waal, I've been sleeping with my sourdough keg for the past two weeks and she's riz to please the eye. I'm full loaded and me louse's back at the spread putting antelope grease on the hubs of the bed wagon. You say the word and we can light out come sunup tomorrow."

Dusty looked at the men who formed a half-circle at the foot of the porch steps. All stood waiting for him to speak.

"All right boys. I'll read you the scriptures here instead of at the spread. Then, if any of you don't like them, you can pull out and save a ride. First, I'm trail boss. And the name, as you likely know, is Dusty Fog.

Miz Holland here's going with us as spread's rep." There was a startled mumble from the men, Dusty waited until it died then carried on:

"She'll be treated as one of the hands. Mark's my segundo, and the Ysabel Kid rides scout, helped by your good friend, Kiowa. Billy Jack or Kiowa will be at point with Mark. The rest of you will ride swing, flank and drag turnabout. The remuda's held at the Rocking H for any of you who need a mount. We'll hold us a choosing match as soon as we get there, taking it in the order you took on. Some of you have rode for Colonel Charlie Goodnight, and you'll know his way. I learned under him and it's my way too. I want to pull out tomorrow so we haven't time to draw up articles. If any of you don't know Colonel Charlie's rules and want to, ask Billy Jack, he'll likely tell you."

The men muttered their agreement to this. Every man had heard of the stringent rules of conduct laid down by the old master of trail-drive work, Colonel Charles Goodnight. They covered the man's life from the time he signed on to when he paid off and protected both his and the owner's interests. They all agreed with the rules, for they knew that their lives would be made easier by following them.

"How about likker, Cap'n?" It was Dude who asked.

"Any toted goes in the wagon and Salt'll hand it out."

This was agreed upon by all the hands. A trail drive was dangerous enough without having a drunk on it. "If that's all, I'll buy a drink. Then we head back for the spread." Dusty stepped aside and the men all started forward across the porch toward the hotel doors.

"Hey, you!"

A man rode toward the porch, a big, heavily built man wearing dirty range clothes and belting a low-tied Navy Colt. He halted the bay he was riding and the other two horses stopped at the same time; they were all nervous-looking animals, the whites of their eyes showing.

"Who's bossing the drive?"

Thora bit her lip as she looked the man over; she had

seen him before somewhere, but couldn't remember where. Dusty was also studying the man and replied. "I am." His attention was now on the muzzles of the horses, not the man.

"You need a wrangler?" The question was directed to Thora more than Dusty. "Man across the street telled me the lady was boss."

"I'm trail boss—and we're full-hired."

"Yeah?" The newcomer's face twisted in a sneer. "Waal, happen the lady'll make you change your mind. See, a friend of her'n telled me to look her up and mention his name."

"Mister"—Dusty's voice was still the same soft drawl but there was a subtle difference to it now—"Miz Holland hired me as trail boss on the understanding that I handled the hiring and firing of the crew. We've got a wrangler and, even if we hadn't, I wouldn't take on a man who uses a ghost cord on his mount."

Thora stared at the horses; she had heard the ranch crew talk about ghost cords. She could see the marks the thin cord had made as it was tied around each horse's tongue and gums, under the lower jaw and the ends carried back to be used as reins. The ghost cord was an instrument of torture and no cowhand worth his salt would use one. The ranch owners also hated the use of the cord, for it either broke the horse's spirit or turned it into a killer.

The man spat into the dust, his hand falling casually toward his side. "Is that right?"

"Try it!" Dusty's flat, barked warning was accompanied by a click as his right-hand gun came out and lined.

The man stared at the long barrel of the Army Colt; it had come out faster than he had ever seen a gun drawn before. Having expected to take the other by surprise, it came as a sudden and nasty shock to him that he had failed, and failed badly.

"All right," he growled, holding his hand well clear of the gun and turning his face to Thora's. "Happen you can talk some sense to your trail boss. Like I said before, this friend of your'n——"

The color drained from Thora's face; she knew who the man was, and who the mysterious friend was. If the Texans heard the name they would never drive for her.

"I'm getting quick sick of you."

Thora hadn't noticed the Ysabel Kid moving forward to her side. He stood there now, his soft-drawled words biting through the other's speech and halting it.

Looking the dark-dressed, innocent-featured youngster over the man made a mistake. He thought he was dealing with some dressed-up button who was still wet behind the ears. "Shy out!" he hissed. "I'm talking to the white——"

The Ysabel Kid went over the hitching rail in a smooth dive which carried the man from his saddle and brought them both crashing to the ground. While the man landed hard on his back, the Ysabel Kid lit down on his feet with an almost catlike agility. Crouching lightly on the balls of his feet, Loncey Dalton Ysabel waited for the man to come up and carry on.

Cursing, he came up, his hand fanning toward the butt of his gun. Even as he did so, Dusty roared out, "Lon! No!"

The sun glinted on eleven-and-a-half inches of razor-sharp steel as the Kid lunged in. His knife made a ripping arc faster than the other man's hand dropped. At the last instant, it swerved and cut through the holster flap. The weight of the Colt swung the severed holster over and the man's hand clawed at an empty space. The gun slid from leather and fell into the dust. Turning, the man leapt toward the rifle stuck in his saddleboot.

Mark Counter vaulted the rail, his hand shooting out to grip the man by the collar and hurl him backward. "Don't be loco, *hombre!*" he snapped. "Lon could just as easy of killed you the first time. Don't tempt him any more—he fails real easy."

The man looked up and saw just what Mark meant. The Ysabel Kid was still standing in that knife-fighter's crouch, his dark face as hard and savage as a Comanche Dog soldier looking for a paleface scalp. He had seen a couple of knife-fighters, this big man, and knew that here was a master hand, one that it would be best to steer clear of.

Slowly he relaxed, his face twisted in a mask of hatred. "All right," he snarled, "I'm going and I won't forget this."

"Happen you won't," the Kid growled back. "Not when things are even you won't."

The man mounted his horse and turning it headed off.

The trail-drive crew had been interested spectators of all this. Billy Jack looked sheepish and holstered his right-hand gun. Sal leered at the miserable-looking rider, he for one being satisfied. His judgment had been vindicated. In a fight, it had been the bowie knife the Ysabel Kid first reached for.

The cowhands trooped into the bar, and Dusty stood by Thora, watching them go. In Texas in the 1870s, a lady didn't enter the barroom and she would have to wait until they returned. She was pleased to note that the diversion had taken the men's minds off the statements the newcomer had made.

Dusty stopped at the door and turned back. "You look worried, Thora. Don't be. That kind of bum always tries a game like that. He'd knew you were from the north and allowed he could get taken on if you thought he knew some friend."

"What do the men make of what he said?"

"About the same as I did. It's your business and none of our'n."

Thora watched Dusty enter the bar and sat down, her legs feeling suddenly weak. The man had known a friend of hers all right—a friend? A man she hated, a man who could lose her every man Dusty had hired. She felt sick and scared, realizing that in the future she might meet this mysterious friend.

Dusty found himself leaning on the bar alongside

Billy Jack. The tall hand still looked as miserable as ever.

"Thought we'd see us some blood out there," Billy Jack remarked, his tones showing that he was disappointed that they hadn't. "The Kid's knife's enough to turn a man's blood cold. Happen you should have let him use it; I just recollected where I last saw that *hombre*. Couldn't place him at first, then I got him."

"Where?"

"With Kliddoe!"

"Kliddoe?" Dusty spat the word out. "You sure on that?"

"Nigh on. Leastwise, he looked powerful like one of the bunch that got clear when ole Shangai Pierce and his crew hit them."

Dusty shook his head, "I can't see that, *amigo*. No Kliddoe man dare show his face in Texas."

"Thought that myself," Billy Jack agreed. "He looked powerful like one of them. He warn't from the south either."

Before Dusty could go further into the matter he was called on by one of the other men to clear up some point of a drive they had been on together. Then, when this was cleared up, he told the men to get their horses and they would head for the Rocking H.

In a saloon along the street, Toon and his foreman sat by the window and watched the cavalcade of men riding by, headed for Rocking H. Toon wasn't in any too good a temper; and it didn't improve when he saw that not only had he failed to stop the Rocking H hiring, but that they had taken the cream of the hands in town.

"What now?" Hendley inquired.

Toon thought it over for a moment and an idea formed in his mind. "Go down to the Doc's and pay off Wren first thing. Then we're going to slow Rocking H down some."

Hendley stiffened. "You ain't going against that bunch with guns, are you?" There was a lamentable lack of enthusiasm in the foreman's tones.

"Nope, brains. You get me that damned half-breed Dan Twofeathers. Get him here real fast. If he don't want to come, tell him I'll have him jailed for slow-elking."

"What have you in mind, Thad?" Hendley had uneasy visions of stampeding the Rocking H herd, and of the consequences. He was brave enough, but the thought of matching lead with that crew was more than he could stand.

"Suppose they was to lose something real important to them?" Toon answered. "Something that'd take them a week or more to replace, and that they can't do without."

"Like what?"

"Like their sourdough keg."

CHAPTER FOUR

Choosing Match

Ben Holland sat in his wheelchair and looked over his range. He was on the porch of his house accompanied by his foreman, a tall, hard-looking man called Sam Starken. Their attention was on the dust cloud which was coming rapidly toward the ranch and along the town trail.

Ben was still healthy looking, and his wide shoulders set back squarely. His time in the wheelchair had left hard, bitter lines round his mouth and there were worry creases around the corners of his eyes. Even Thora didn't know how worried Ben had been since his return from Dodge. The worries of the ranch were not great, Sam Starken and the crew being able to handle anything that came up on the home range. Getting the herd to market was another thing though. That herd meant badly needed money to the Rocking H, money that couldn't be got in any other way.

"That's Miz Thora," Sam Starken growled. "Got what looks like a full crew along with her."

Starken pushed his boss to the edge of the porch and Ben felt worried as he watched the men coming toward the ranch. Thora wasn't experienced in matters of this sort, and there was no telling what sort of men she would take on. At best, he hoped that they might get enough hands to allow him to send half the crew along and keep the new men on Rocking H to handle the cattle.

The first thing that became obvious was that the riders Thora was bringing were at least all good horsemen. As they came nearer, both men began to recognize some of them.

"Damned if the gal ain't a living wonder," Ben growled huskily. "She's done took on Kiowa and Billy Jack both. There's a pair to draw to."

Starken gulped hard: he knew the two men by reputation, but there were certain others he knew as friends. He could hardly believe the evidence of his eyes. "Got Red Tolliver there, 'n' Duke Lane. If that ain't Basin Jones, I'll swan! Took with Kiowa and Billy Jack them three'd make a dandy full house."

Ben could not think how Thora had managed to hire such men; even the small man on the big paint had the air of a tophand. This last rider looked vaguely familiar to Ben, but he couldn't place the face.

The party came to a halt before the ranch house and fanned out into a rough half-circle. Ben looked around and felt even more amazement as the correct caliber of the riders became apparent to his range-wise eyes. They must represent the pick of the town; in fact, they would be hard to match in Texas.

The handsome, blonde giant on the blood bay swung down and turned to help Thora from the wagon. She came forward and the small man on the paint rode up. "Howdy, Cousin Ben," he greeted. "Uncle Devil heard you needed some help and sent me along to ride trail boss for you."

Then Ben knew who the small man was and knew how these riders came to be here. "Howdy, Cousin Dusty." He held out his hand as the small man dismounted. "Real obliged to you for coming. This here's my foreman, Sam Starken."

"Howdy, Sam." Dusty appraised the man with one quick, all-seeing glance, then got down to business. "Miss Thora allows the herd is ready to move. Happen you'll let me take a horse from your remuda. I'll head out and look it over."

"Sure, Dusty." Starken liked a man who got right straight down to business. "We'll head out soon as you're ready."

"Mark, Billy Jack," Dusty barked out. "I want you

along with me. Lon, you take four of the hands and roust out the cable from the bed wagon. Lil Jackie, Tarbrush, I want the remuda handled as soon as I get back."

The Kid turned to Thora and sighed. "That's how you tell a trail boss, ma'am. He can't rest hisself and it surely hurts him to see the help rest."

Dusty looked his pard over in some disgust. "You've rested most of all your wicked and sinful young life. Time comes when a man has to start you in to working."

Dusty, Mark and Billy Jack each cut a horse from the Rocking H remuda, saddled it and headed, with the foreman, to look over the herd. Thora went to stand by her husband and watched them go. "Did I do all right?"

"Honey, nobody could have done better."

She flushed at the praise, then shook her head. "I'm not too happy about either Billy Jack or Kiowa. I wouldn't have taken them on. But Dusty did and I promised not to interfere. Do you know either of them?"

"Heard of them both," Ben answered, a grin flickering round the corner of his lips in a way which Thora hadn't seen since his return from Dodge. "Billy Jack rode segundo for Shangai Pierce that last drive, when they cut Kliddoe's gang to doll rags. Kiowa used to ride for Ole Devil Hardin and for Clay Allison. They're tophands, both of them, and they could get took on as segundo most any place they chose to go. There aren't many better trail drivers in the West."

Thora turned her attention to what the other men were doing; some of the men were by the corral, examining the horses of the remuda, while others were helping unload their bedrolls from the wagon. The Kid and four men were at the second wagon and taking out a thick rope.

Turning back, she told her husband what had happened in town. Ben listened without a word, only speaking when she asked, "How did Toon know I'd hired Dusty? In fact, I hadn't even told Dusty he was hired."

"You didn't have to tell him. When a hand throws his bedroll into the wagon he's hired and part of the crew." Ben replied. "I'm not sorry that Dusty didn't down Thad—he ain't all that bad a *hombre.*"

"The other man who came," Thora licked her lips before she went on, "I recognized him. His name is Blount and he rode for Kliddoe. I was afraid he was going to tell the men about me. The Kid stopped him just in time."

Ben gripped her hand, seeing the fear in her eyes. "Honey, you don't need to go north with the herd. You know that Kliddoe's out again and that Dusty won't let him collect any head tax."

"I know." The little she had seen of Dusty Fog told her that. "But, if it comes to the worst, I may be able to do something to help."

Starken escorted Dusty, Mark and Billy Jack out to the bottomlands where half the crew were holding the herd. Dusty looked the herd over from a distance; then they rode nearer and circled around. The cattle were all steers, long horned, half-wild and well meated up. They would stand the long drive north with no trouble and, given luck, would reach Dodge City in first-class shape.

"Be around three thousand head?" Dusty guessed.

"We road-branded three thousand, two hundred, but happen a few more will have got in."

Mark had made an even more careful study of the cattle than Dusty had.

More than the trail boss, the segundo had to be concerned with the cattle. Dusty, as trail boss, would have many problems on his mind; he had to handle the men, the remuda, any emergency that might come up. Mark was the man who would be mostly concerned with the cattle themselves.

"Look real well, Sam," he finally remarked. "You don't get so much tick trouble this far north?"

"Not much and none this time of the year," Sam replied. "They'll likely not die off afore you get to Dodge."

"Reckon your boys can handle the night herd for us, tonight, Sam?" Dusty inquired as they headed back toward the ranch. "I'd like to give the trail crew a decent night's sleep."

"Sure, I aimed to keep half the crew out. Don't figure Thad Toon be loco enough to try scattering the herd, but he might."

"If he does," Dusty growled, "he'll surely wish he'd never been born."

The Ysabel Kid saw Dusty coming back and called, "Set up that cable over here."

The four hands took up the heavy rope and carried it to the place Lon had pointed out. One man was at each end, and the two others pulled the center back to form a loose U shape. This was the only corral they would use all the way north. To someone who didn't know western horses this might look like a flimsy enclosure, but every horse in the remuda had learned early and painfully what a rope was.

Little Jackie and Tarbrush sat their mounts on either side of the corral gate as the Rocking H wrangler opened it and allowed the horses to come out. The two riders came on either side and, without fuss or bother, hazed the horses into the cable corral. The horses halted and milled around, and the four rope-holders shook the cable a few times just to remind the remuda what it was.

"Boy handles the remuda all right," Mark drawled as they watched the corralling of the horses.

"Sure, time he gets to Dodge he'll have made a hand, and next time he goes, he'll be ready to ride the herd," Dusty answered. Then, he frowned and growled, "Look!"

A big black gelding cut back from the milling horses, out of the corral, and broke for the open range. Mark started his horse forward but Jackie had already turned it back toward the corral.

"Red, take the cable over there a piece. Jackie, Tarbrush, bring them in again."

Red Tolliver, at the cable, acknowledged the order with a wave. Then he lowered his end of the cable. The other holders let the rope go down and backed off to re-form the loose U a couple of hundred yards away. Again the horses were brought in and, once more, the black broke back out.

"All right, move the cable again." Dusty sounded grim.

On the porch, Thora and Ben were watching. The rancher explained to his wife all that was happening. They saw the new cable set up again; the remuda was driven in and then the black broke out once more. Ben's hands gripped the arms of his chair and, in a roar that was echoed by every watching man, he yelled, "Takes his toes up!"

Dusty had reached forward and unstrapped his rope as the third coralling commenced. When the black broke back out, he was ready—and so was the wiry dun roping horse he had borrowed for the ride to the herd. A touch sent the little horse leaping forward. It knew just what it was supposed to do as it moved to the rear and left of the big black.

The sixty-foot rope came alive in Dusty's hands, a medium-sized loop building, forming and sailing out. The noose passed across the horse and slightly ahead of its right shoulder, then dropped into position to trap the feet. Dusty gave his rope an inward twist as the noose dropped. This turned the loop to hit against the horse's knees, and then trap the feet.

Up to that moment, the black ran blithely on, confident that it was the master of its destiny and the two-legged things were impotent against it. Then its forelegs suddenly locked tight together and it landed with a bone-jarring thud, trapped by Dusty's well-executed forefoot throw.

Thora leapt to her feet as the horse smashed down, her face shocked and angry, "Did you see that?"

"Sure did, honey. That Dusty can handle a rope."

"But he could have broken that horse's neck!" she gasped. "It was a dangerous thing to do."

"Reckon Dusty'd rather have bust the horse's neck than have him break out like that. Breaking out's the worst thing a remuda horse can do. It's catching and can ruin the remuda." Ben watched Dusty release the black and point out another place for the cable corral to be set up. "I'll bet he doesn't break back out again."

Thora watched the shifting of the cable again and, once more, the horses were driven in. This time, she noticed, the big black didn't try and break back.

Tarbrush and Little Jackie rode around the cable corral and the Negro turned to the youngster. "You watch real careful now, Jackie boy," he warned. "They's going to have their choosing match and we've got to know who all has what."

Dusty rode forward and looked round the milling horses. A wiry, smallish bay caught his eye and he spun his rope up to catch the horse, then lead it out. Releasing the bay, he headed back and picked out the rest of his mounts. The other hands watched the choosing, and noted with approval that their trail boss was taking the rough string. Every horse he picked bore the look of a fighter, a horse it would take a good man to handle.

In a choosing match the men took turn in order of seniority with the ranch; in this case, in the order they had been hired in town. Mark had second choice; he picked out the biggest horses, five of them, including the big black. These joined Dusty's mounts in the care of the wranglers and the Ysabel Kid rode out.

Ignoring the remuda, the Kid went straight to the ranch house and halted before the porch. "Ben, you got anything with a mite of speed? I don't want to take cowhorses for riding scout."

"Got just what you do want, *amigo*," Ben replied. "Comanche war relay that I bought off a brave. They're in the small corral, at the back of the spread. You go and look them over."

There was joy in the Kid's heart as he headed round the house and looked over three horses in the small corral. Riding scout was a dangerous enough task any time, and the horses a man had could mean the difference between living to be old and ornery and making a hair decoration on some scalp-hunting buck's belt.

The three horses were small, rough-coated and wiry,
yet they were alike in one thing. Each was powerfully
muscled and looked as if it could run forever. More,
they had been trained as a warrior's relay by a tribe who
were horsemen without equal. The three horses had been
trained to run together, their rider on one and the other
two following him. All in all, they were just what the
Ysabel Kid wanted when he rode scout for the herd.
Opening the corral gate, the Kid drove the three horses
out and headed them toward the group of horses being
held by Little Jackie and Tarbrush.

Little Jackie watched the increasing remuda and felt
nervous. He could see there was much more to handling
a trail-drive remuda than there had been to working as
ranch wrangler. However he would have one advantage
in that the remuda would not increase in size much; on
the drive, they would not have many visitors, while, at
a ranch, there was always a chance that someone would
ride up and add his string to the wrangler's cares. The
youngster watched the horses and realized that he would
have to remember every man's mount and know all their
habits. He would have to learn, and learn fast, which
were the bunch-quitters, the fighters, the nervous and
the mean horses, if he was to do his work properly.

Each man took the horses he would need and added
them to the trail remuda. Then Dusty picked out ten
spare horses. The ranch wrangler cut out Thora's mount
for her and added them to the bunch belonging to the
trail crew.

The sun was going down but the men still had time
to ride out some of their mounts and get the bedsprings
out of their backs. Each man cut out one of the horses,
saddled it and then hopped aboard, hoping for the best.

What followed was a display of riding that would
have drawn big crowds in the East. Here, it drew only
sarcastic jeers and cheerful advice from the watchers.

The horses bucked, leapt, sunfished and tried to get
rid of their riders; occasionally one was successful but

the man got back to his feet and mounted again. To let a horse end a winner gave it bad habits and encouraged it to try again.

"Ketch my saddle!" Billy Jack went off his horse and howled the time-honored cry as he lit on the ground.

It was Dusty who obliged by returning the doleful one's saddle along with the ranch horse. "You resting already?" he asked.

"Why sure, likewise wondering when we're going to see the trail boss ride any of his string."

Dusty laughed, tossed Billy Jack the reins and then rode to the remuda to cut out one of his string. He took the conceit out of the horse in chunks and then went on to do the same with the others.

The trail hands were correct in their guess. Dusty had taken the rough string; every horse here was a fighter as well as a trained cowhorse. The hands also had their views confirmed; Captain Fog was the best horseman of them all and he would have little or no trouble with his mounts.

The night was coming in fast when Dusty rode the last of his string to the side of the two chuck wagons and looked down at the cook and his fat, cheerful young louse.

Salt was unaware that he was being watched and proudly displayed a five-gallon wooden keg to his louse. "This here's the best danged sourdough keg you'll ever see," he said proudly. "You kin sleep with it tonight and make sure you take care of it."

Hobie accepted the keg reverently, for he knew the value the trail crew would set by it. The sourdough keg was the most important item the chuck wagon carried and was Salt's most treasured possession. In the keg was fermenting dough, ready for bread—or biscuit-making; it took time to prepare and without it the crew would be on short rations.

Wrapping the keg in blankets, Hobie asked, "When you going to let me make up a keg of my own?"

"Happen you're careful and l'arn well, in about ten, fifteen years." Salt answered, then looked up. "Howdy, Cap'n."

"You pair all ready to roll first thing tomorrow?"

"Allus ready," Salt replied. "And, comes Dodge, we'll slap ole Sam Snenton's brand on this here ole keg."

"Happen you haven't poisoned us all before that," Dusty scoffed. "You keep them fool knobheads back where they belong and don't crowd the remuda. Iffen you don't, I'll likely slap my brand somewhere and it won't be on a keg."

Before Salt could think up any reply to either suggestion that he would let his mules get too close to the remuda, or that he might poison the crew, Dusty had turned the horse and headed for the remuda.

The two wranglers watched the trail boss come up and Dusty pointed toward the stream behind the ranch house. "Hold them down here tonight," he ordered as he stripped off the saddle, then turned the horses in with the others. "Keep my paint and Mark's blood bay away from the others."

"Yes, sah, Cap'n." Tarbrush rolled his eyes and waved his hand toward the Kid's big white as it grazed away from the others. "I surely hopes Massa Kid ain't going to put his hoss in with the rest of the remuda."

"He isn't." Dusty could see that his nighthawk had a keen eye for the character of a horse. "He'll stay clear—and Jackie, don't you ever try and touch that white, happen you want to keep both arms."

"Boy," Tarbrush waited until Dusty strolled away with his saddle slung over his shoulder, "them is the truest words you'll ever hear. That hoss there looks meaner than two starving devil-cats."

Ben and Thora entertained the three young Texans at the house that night. After the meal was over, they sat in the dining room and talked. Thora brought in coffee for the men and stopped as she heard them discussing the happenings of the day. She came in as they were

mentioning the man who had tried to get taken on as
wrangler.

"Wisht Billy Jack'd spoken sooner about him being
a Kliddoe man," the Kid said mildly. "I'd have spoken
loving words with him."

Thora frowned; she didn't want to let them get thinking about the man again, so she asked, "How does Kliddoe work?"

"Ole Yellerdawg?" The Kid sniffed. "He takes head
tax on the herd."

"Head tax?"

"Sure, it's an old game," Mark explained. "Came out
when the first drives went north after the war. He used
to come on the herd backed by fifty or so men and claim
he'd been sent out by the Governor to take head tax on
the herds. He had a real legal-looking bit of paper and
his men backed it up. It worked for a spell—either the
drives paid off or they fought and they were outnumbered. Then Stone Hart and his Wedge crew called his
bluff, that was over Abilene way. They drove over the
Kliddoe bunch and got through. Kliddoe went into hiding
after that; the Governor came out flat-footed and said he
wasn't aware that Kliddoe worked for him. Waal, we got
word that Kliddoe started after your drive last year, but
he ran into bad luck. Shangai Pierce's scout found where
they were at and, when Kliddoe tried to take the herd,
they had him whipsawed. Kliddoe and some of his men
got clear. Shangai and his boys gave the rest a coat of
molasses and feathers and turned them adrift. They
missed Kliddoe though—he got clear."

"Trust ole Yellerdawg!" the Kid sneered. "Regular
ole Yankee hero, him. Real loyal blue-belly."

All eyes went to the dark youngster, Ben and Thora
wondering at the vicious hardness in his voice. Thora
wondered where the Ysabel Kid had known the Yankee
leader, Jethro Kliddoe. "Do you know him?" she asked.

"Never met him. Came across a real good friend of
his in the war though."

"What happened?" Thora had asked before she realized that she had gone beyond the bounds of frontier friendliness.

"He died happy, I guess." The Kid rolled a smoke as he replied. "One day I'm going to meet ole Yellerdawg—and, when I do I'll make him wish his maw never met his pappy the one time she did!"

Dusty and Mark remembered other times when the name of Kliddoe had been mentioned. Every time that same alum-bitter snarl had come into their pard's tones, although he had never told them why he hated Kliddoe.

"Reckon we'd best turn in," Dusty remarked. "You'd best get some sleep, Cousin Thora, likely you'll be needing."

"What time will we be leaving tomorrow?" she inquired as the three Texans rose.

"Soon after sunup as we can," Dusty replied. "See you in the morning."

The rest of the trail crew were in their bedrolls already; they were getting a good night's sleep for what might be the last time until the drive was over.

Dusty, Mark and the Kid spread their rolls away from the others—not through any sense of superiority, but because they didn't want to disturb the rest. Dusty looked around the area, then snapped the clips of his tarp and went to sleep.

The Ysabel Kid woke. There was no half-waking, half-sleeping period for him, just a swift transition from sleep to full alertness. He didn't move, just lay still waiting to locate the sound that had wakened him. It wasn't the distant sound of the nighthawk riding his rounds; that sound had never stopped and hadn't wakened him. It wasn't the stamping and movement of the trail crews' night horses. Slowly he emerged from his bedroll, his old Dragoon in his right hand. The sound which had wakened him came from the dark bulk of the two wagons and it was toward these he made his way. The rest of the crew were still all asleep around the dying embers of their fire.

The few seconds' delay caused the Kid to curse himself several times in the next few hours.

From the chuck wagon sounded a muffled yell, then a thud. Dark shapes moved from the rear of the wagon. The Kid wasted no time; he darted forward and barked, "Hold it!"

There were three shapes. Leaping from the wagon, they ran into the blackness toward a smaller, darker shape—either a buggy or a buckboard, the Kid guessed. One of the men threw something into the back of the wagon and then leapt aboard. The other two grabbed horses and all set off away fast.

The old Dragoon boomed in the darkness, flame lancing from the muzzle. He knew he had missed and raced to the side of the wagon; but he was too late to get in another shot.

Men yelled and shouted and the camp was awake. Dusty was the first man to join the Kid. "What the hell, Lon?"

A groan from the back of the wagon stopped any reply. Dusty and the Kid went to the tailboard and Dusty lit a match. Hobie lay on the bed of the wagon, blood running from a gash in his scalp. The blankets were all thrown about and, in the last instant before Dusty had to throw the spent match to one side, he saw what was missing.

The small Texan cursed savagely. The sourdough keg was gone.

CHAPTER FIVE

Mr. Toon Learns a Lesson

Dusty took in the sight and made his decision right away. Even as the other men gathered round, asking questions and yelling for lights, he snapped, "Lon, Kiowa, get it back."

Neither man wasted time in obeying this casually given order to do the almost impossible. Kiowa didn't even know what was missing, but he didn't wait to ask about it. Indian smart, he had his night horse staked near to hand, saddled, and only needing the girths drawn tight. He ran for the horse even as the Kid's shrill whistle shattered the night and brought the big white horse running to him.

Mark came up. He tossed the Kid his gunbelt and then stood back, holding the rifle. He knew that in a delicate matter of this nature, Mr. O. F. Winchester's .44 brainchild was of as much use as old Colonel Sam's heavy weight thumb-buster, or Mr. James Black's razor-edged bowie knife.

Salt was by the chuck wagon. He howled in fury when he saw that his precious keg was gone. Running to where the night horses were tethered, he grabbed one without asking who might own it. Tightening the girths, he swung into the saddle and headed for the wagon to get his old Sharp's carbine. . . .

The Kid was afork his white without bothering with such refinements as saddle or bridle. He thrust the Dragoon into his waistband and strapped on the belt, then holstered the revolver and caught the rifle Mark tossed him. Then he and Kiowa lit out into the night.

Salt tore by the crew, waving his rifle and yelling, "I'll get 'em."

"They're on our side," Mark called after him.

The rest of the trail crew whooped their approval, even Basin Jones who owned the horse Salt had taken. Dusty turned to the men and gave his orders: "Fix young Hobie's head, Dude," he snapped. "Rest of you get back to sleep."

Thora came up wearing a long house coat and Indian moccasins on her feet. "What happened?" she asked.

"Somebody stole the sourdough keg."

Thora felt like sobbing; this was the final blow. To get so near to starting the herd and then to find that they would be delayed until Salt could make up another keg seemed like the height of injustice to her. She was near to tears as she said, "Then we can't start tomorrow."

Dusty looked off into the darkness to where, growing fainter all the time, he could hear the sound of horses running. "We'll pull out at dawn just like we said we would. Somebody thought they could slow us down by taking the keg. They were wrong."

"But we can't manage without it?" Thora objected, having heard how important the keg was.

"We'll have to," Dusty replied. "Besides I sent Lon and Kiowa after the men who took it. Likely they'll get it back, happen old Salt don't get too much in their way."

"Salt?"

"Sure. He lit out of here afork old Basin's night hoss like the devil after a yearling." Dusty turned to where, by the light of a lantern, Dude was attending to the cook's louse. "How is he?"

"Reckon he'll live," Dude answered. "Who d'you reckon did it?"

"I'm reckoning, not saying." Dusty grinned at Thora as he replied. "Know one thing though. Happen Lon and Kiowa find them, they'll surely wish they'd never done it at all."

"But they can't find the men in the dark," Thora put in.

The same sentiments were being expressed about a mile from the ranch, where Salt finally caught up with the other two, who had stopped their horses and were seated silently. "Can we find them?" Salt growled.

"Yeah, Kid," Kiowa sounded dubious, "my Grandpappy's kin were fair hands at reading sign, but they never tried it at night."

"Kiowas never was wuth a cuss at reading sign day or night," the Kid jeered back. "But us Comanches are some different. Anyways I'm not trying to read sign, I'm letting this ole Nigger hoss of mine do it."

"Dangnab it, if I ain't see-rounded by Injun varmints," Salt cursed. "Get to it, damn ye, or do you want to take time out to get your warpaint on. That there keg's too dang good to be taken by any robbing skunk."

The Ysabel Kid allowed his big white to follow the sounds which were too faint for even him or Kiowa to locate. He rode at the head of the party, sitting the horse alert and ready for instant action. The other two followed, confident that the big white stallion would not only locate the men they were after, but would also steer them clear of any ambush.

The time passed slowly, and the men rode on, only Salt being aware of the direction in which they were traveling. He began to mumble out curses as he became more sure of the direction they were taking.

The Kid and Kiowa ignored him for a time. Then, drawing their horses to a halt, they studied the cook. "What're you on at now?" the Kid finally asked.

"Toon's spread's down thisways. It must have been him that took the keg."

"Me, I figgered it was Santanta," Kiowa scoffed.

"Naw, I reckoned it was ole Dingus James'd come up from Clay County just especial, that fool keg being so valuable," the Kid put in.

Salt spluttered in silent fury, the entire conversation having been carried out in whispers. He swore by several sacred objects that two certain Injuns would suffer for those insults to his beloved keg when they got back to the spread.

The ranch house loomed black against the surrounding darkness, a single small light showing that folk were out and about. Off from the ranch house, some half a mile away, was another larger, darker mass.

"That's real lucky," the Kid remarked, "he's holding his herd right close up."

They rode their horses nearer to the ranch, keeping to a steady walk and making as little noise as possible. The Kid halted and allowed the other two to come alongside him. The door of the house opened and a man came out, going to the buggy and the two horses which could be seen outside.

"Gets on Injun style," Kiowa remarked as the man mounted one of the horses and headed off into the darkness.

Salt too had noted the right-hand mounting of the horse and decided that a half-bred gentleman called Dan Twofeathers had best start looking for a new home real soon.

The door closed again and only the light in the window showed that Thad Toon was still not abed as befitting a man with work to do the following morning.

"Le's go down'n'get 'em," Salt growled.

"That's real smart," the Kid scoffed. "And, afore we gets in there, they could likely bust up that fool keg and throw it on the stove."

"Holding their herd over thatways, we could happen——" Kiowa began.

"Yeah." The Kid had an idea; it was audacious, but, given some luck, it might work. He went on speaking rapidly, but Salt couldn't understand a word.

The two horses started forward again and Salt spat out an angry curse as he realized he didn't know what was happening, "Hey, you danged Injuns. What you fixing to do?"

The Ysabel Kid stopped his horse and twisted round,

then lifted his hand in a mocking peace sign. "Stay right here, white brother. Keepum bad paleface inside stone wickiup." He paused and a wicked grin played around his lips. "Happen you can hit the house from up here with that rusted-up ole Beecher's Bible."

Looking down at his highly prized Sharp's carbine, Salt prepared to defend its virtues. Before he could open his mouth the other two had faded into the blackness.

Sim Hogan of the Double T liked to ride night herd; it gave him a chance to whistle without anyone asking him to stop. He was a keen and ardent whistler, though there were certain members of the Double T crew who, with no appreciation for the arts, insisted that he was out of tune most of the time. Out here, riding along one half of the sleeping herd, he could whistle to his heart's content—for the cattle never complained and he didn't go near enough to his pard, Kenny, to hear his views.

Halfway along the line of Sim's patrol stood an old cottonwood tree, a very useful growth and one he much approved of. A man could ride behind the thick old trunk and, hidden from the herd, light up a smoke without risking scaring the cattle and starting a stampede.

Thinking about the use of the tree reminded Sim that it was some time since last he had a smoke. Turning his horse's head toward the tree, he steered it under the thick branches and stopped the movement. Sim bent forward and took out his makings. He had just started to roll a smoke when, from the branch above, something lashed down and thudded on to his head. Sim slipped sideways from his saddle and fell to the ground without a sound. Before the cowhand hit the earth a dark shape dropped into the saddle of the startled horse. Strong hands gripped the reins and a soft, soothing voice stopped it from spooking.

Riding the other flank of the herd, Kenny saw a horse coming toward him. Thinking Sim wanted to talk, the cowhand rode to meet him, noting idly that the whistling was in tune at last. He grinned, then the grin froze on his face as he got an uneasy feeling all was not well here. The proof of his feeling became more clear to him as the other man rode toward him.

Sim might have learned, in a sudden and miraculous way, to whistle in tune; but he would hardly have changed his riding style to do it. Even if he had changed the way he sat a horse, he couldn't have changed his clothing in the short time he was behind the tree.

Kenny's hand dropped to his hip. He spoke softly, "Sim?"

"Guess again!" The soft drawled reply was backed by a sound, the sound a Colt made when it came back to full cock.

The rider was close enough in now for Kenny to see that he was a tall, young man dressed all in black. In the stranger's hand, as Kenny had rightly guessed, was a Colt. The Double T cowhand had little but contempt for old Colonel Sam's second Hartford Dragoon model revolver, considering it both over-heavy and out of date. This contempt did not extend to open criticism when one was lined on his belly at hardly any range at all.

"What the——?" he began.

"Silence is golden, friend," the stranger replied. "We wouldn't want to go and wake up all them poor lil ole cows, now would we?"

Before Kenny could make any reply the stranger gave a low whistle and a riderless white horse came out of the darkness, followed by a tall man riding a big buckskin. A man Kenny thought he recognized. A man who apparently could see better than the Double T man in the dark.

"Howdy, Kenny boy." It was the voice of Kiowa all right. "What now, Kid?"

It took Kenny a moment to realize that it was the dark boy on Sim's horse Kiowa was addressing.

"Take his gun," the Kid replied.

Kenny suffered this indignity without argument; he did not know who the dark man called Kid was, but he did know Kiowa. They had once ridden for the same brand and Kenny knew better than to fool with the dark,

dangerous man called Kiowa. He noticed that although
Kiowa had a rifle in his saddleboot, he also carried a
second—and wondered why all the armament? He saw
when the other man changed from Sim's mount to the
big white, Kiowa tossed the rifle to him.

"Never knowed you was a rustler, Kiowa," he remarked as the other man striped the caps from the nipples
of his gun, then dropped it back into his holster.

"Just l'arning from the Kid here. We'll head back and
pick up your bunkie."

Kenny stiffened as the import of the words hit him.
His voice was brittle and angry. "Is Sim dead?" he asked.

"Have a lump on his head come morning," the Ysabel
Kid replied. "I don't reckon he'll take much hurt, but
it evens us for our louse."

By the time they reached the tree, Kenny had learned
about the raid and the stealing of Rocking H's sourdough
keg. As a loyal member of the Double T, he was both
amused and delighted at the ingenious way his boss had
attempted to slow down the Rocking H trail-herd. Then
the amusement and pleasure died off as he thought of
what would have happened if any of the other spread's
crew had been killed in the attempt. Kenny knew from
experience what Kiowa would have done; he didn't think
the other man would have been any less easy in extracting
his revenge.

"What you fixing in to do with us?" he asked.

"Waal now," the Kid answered, "we just happens to
want you to take a message in to your boss."

Inside Toon's room at the ranch the light was still on.
The keg and a full bottle of whisky stood side by side
on the table. Toon was at peace with the world and he
grinned at his foreman as he poured out two large drinks.
"That went off real neat, Joel."

"Yeah, but comes daylight the Ysabel Kid and some
of the others'll be reading sign and coming out here."

"We can handle them." There was confidence in
Toon's tones. "The boys'll fight if they have to. Rocking
H can't prove we took their keg and I sent into Granite

for the law. Telled Dan Twofeathers to tell the town marshal to get out here and lend a hand. Rocking H'll be on my land and he'll have to turn them off. If they gets here before the law, we'll bust their keg and burn it."

Hendley relaxed. He looked the keg over and slapped it with a hard hand. "Say, let's us hide this keg out until they've gone. Then we can take it north with us and leave it at Sam Snenton's place. The Rocking H won't never dare show their faces in Dodge again."

Toon whooped in delight as he saw what would happen. The Rocking H would be the laughing stock of the range country, the crew who had lost their sourdough keg. Ben Holland would never hear the end of it.

"Yeah," he agreed. "We'll do just that. It'll even us some with Ben Holland and his crew."

"Kid might not be able to trail us." Hendley's optimism rose as he drained down the drink. "The wind gets up come dawn, it'll blow the sign right off."

"Yeah." The optimism was contagious and Toon sat back with a happy beam on his face. "Rocking H, the crew that lost their sourdough keg!"

The rosy dreams were shattered as the door was thrown open and Kenny came in, half dragging, half carrying his pard from the night herd.

Toon watched Kenny lay his pard on the floor and straighten up, then yelled, "Kenny, what the hell are you doing here, away from the herd?"

The reply came from a different source, not from Kenny. It came from the darkness outside in the sound of a wild yell.

"Hi, Toon! Hey, Toon! You've got our keg in there, we've got your herd out here. Do we trade?"

Toon and Hendley stared at each other as if they couldn't believe the evidence of their ears. Then Toon growled, "Kenny, get into the bunkhouse 'n'——"

"Happen there's any evil designs in there," the voice went on, "we got Brother Kiowa out here lined on the hawgpen door, right ready 'n' willing to ventilate any gent who shows his fool head. Out front, ole Pastor Ballew's got him a right true bead on the door with his rusted-up ole Sharps."

"Leave us also remember them poor, dear, lil ole cows," Kiowa's voice came to them from the rear of the building, "which same're like to be up and headed to hell and gone comes shooting and you getting out of your house."

Toon and his men knew this, even without Kiowa's friendly reminder. Like Kiowa said, come shooting the herd would be up and running. Even if it wasn't, Kiowa or one of the others could slip away while the remainder pinned down the ranch crew, it would only need one man to scatter the herd. Rocking H might be delayed by the loss of their keg, but not as much as the Double T would be. That herd would be scattered and would take some finding. It would call for another, complete roundup to gather them in again and cut the road-branded stock from the other cattle.

Crossing to the window, Toon looked out. It was still some time to dawn and, in the blackness, he could see nothing of the men who were laying up out there. "How do we know you won't scatter the herd when I've sent the keg out?"

"You don't," the comforting reply came back promptly enough. "But you don't have any choice. Time you fight your way out, there won't be any herd left."

"He's right, damn him!" Hendley spat the words out bitterly. "Even if the marshal gets here by dawn, they'll have scattered the herd."

"Send it out, Toon." Even at this range, they could tell there was a harder note in the Kid's voice. "We're getting quick sick of waiting."

"Send your ramrod out with it," Kiowa's voice went on. "I ain't stampeded a herd since the last time, and that's some too long."

Toon stamped across the room, his face black with anger. He picked up the whisky bottle, and with a savage curse, smashed it on to the floor. Then he gripped the keg and for a wild moment, was tempted to smash it, or to empty it out. Sanity came back to him; he knew that the Rocking H men held the whiphand and that he had to give in. If he damaged or emptied the keg, they would find out soon enough and the revenge would be small compared with the loss of his herd.

Hendley took the keg from the table, warning Kenny to keep the rest of the ranch crew quiet and not let them do anything foolish like shooting at the watchers. An idea was forming in his mind as he carried the keg to the door. Kenny opened the door and allowed the fore-man to go out. He was told to shut it again and keep it shut.

It was dark now, darker than it had been all the night, as Hendley stepped off the porch and stood allowing his eyes to become accustomed to the darkness.

A man came toward him, a dark shape emerging from the black of the night; Hendley was pleased to see it was old Salt Ballew, not either the Ysabel Kid or Kiowa. The half-formed plan was far safer now. All Hendley had to do was wait until the cook came close, then drop the keg and grab him. With the Kid, or Kiowa, that would have been deadly dangerous; but even though Salt was a tough handful, he would be easier meat.

Grinning, Hendley moved forward to meet Salt. He would show the Rocking H how the game should be played. They might be smart and have the best cards, but shortly they were going to lose their ace in the hole and be left sat with a dead hand.

Something touched Hendley's back, something with a sharp point. A soft voice said, "Far enough, friend. Set her down."

Hendley almost dropped the keg, his startled gasp bursting out unchecked. He let the keg fall to the ground and then stood very still. That thing sticking in his back might only be a sharpened bit of whittling wood, *might* be. It might also be, and was, eleven and a half inches of razor-sharp steel from Mr. James Black's Arkansas forge. It was the Ysabel Kid's bowie knife and was held in a position just handy to remove his kidneys if he even blinked too hard.

Salt came up and bent over the keg. He rasped a match on his pants and, in the glare, looked it over with loving care. Hendley gulped and offered a silent prayer that his orders regarding no shooting were obeyed without question. He knew that if anyone shot at Salt his own life was due to come to a painful and messy end. Joel Hendley was brave enough in the face of gunmen, but that wasn't a gun in his back. The thought of the knife going home unnerved him.

"She all right, Salt?" the Kid inquired.

"She be," Salt sounded grim. "But if she hadn't been I'd've surely killed you in inches, Joel Hendley."

"Back off, Salt," the Ysabel Kid warned. "And take that danged fool keg along with you. We'll be long gone afore they can get after us."

Salt grabbed the keg and departed fast. Hendley watched the cook go, then heard a fresh sound. It was the noise of a horse retreating into the night. Soon after, there was another commotion down by the corral. Once more, hoof-beats sounded. This time, of many horses. Hendley cursed under his breath as he realized what was happening. The remuda was being driven off onto the open range.

"Left you two tied, for the night herd," the Kid explained. "Rest won't scatter that far, I reckon."

"Reckon so. Thanks for the two."

"That's all right," the Kid answered as he lifted Hendley's gun from its holster and tossed it to one side, "Dusty'd want it that way. Who war it hit our cook's louse?"

"The 'breed." Hendley was wondering if there was any chance of taking the Kid by surprise. The knife moved from his back and he stiffened just a little, ready to try and make a move.

"Yield not to evil temptations, brother," that soft voice warned. "It'd only get you hurt real bad. She's still out ready."

Hendley relaxed again. His only hope was to stall for time and wait for a chance when the Kid came to take his departure. "Your man hurt bad?" he inquired.

"Nope."

"Good, the 'breed didn't have to hit him. I was for taking a quirt to Twofeathers, but we was in a hurry. Take it kind that you didn't hurt young Sim real bad."

The Kid whistled shrilly, then replied, "Had Hobie been hurt, we'd have been some less friendly."

Hooves thundered and a big white horse raced around the side of the house, traveling at a dead run. Hendley knew this was the chance he had been waiting for. He spun round ducking and flailing a looping blow which he hoped would catch the young man. His fist hit only empty air and the force of his blow staggered him off balance.

The Kid stood, not just behind, but some distance back. He had been as keenly aware of the danger at the time of his departure as had Hendley, and to avert it moved back silently. He looked down with a mocking smile and drawled, "You been learning from beginners, friend."

Saying this he whirled and ran forward, caught the mane of the big white and vaulted aboard, sheathed his knife and sent his mount racing away into the night.

Hendley dived for his gun and caught it up. He came up to one knee and lined it, easing back the hammer. Then he shook his head, lowered the hammer again and rose, shoving the gun back into leather. " 'Twouldn't be right, not after they left us two horses for the night herd."

Toon, Kenny and some more of the crew came out of the house as they heard the sound of the horse. They listened as Hendley, with many a lurid curse, told of how the Ysabel Kid had handled the entire business. They cursed the black-dressed, baby-faced rider from the Rio Grande, but there was admiration for a master in their curses.

"Get the crew out," Toon howled at the end. "We'll take out after them and get the——"

"Get nothing, we *won't*," Hendley contradicted. "For one thing, there ain't but two horses left—and them for the night herd. For another, and more important, them's the Ysabel Kid and Kiowa out there. The man who goes after that pair in the dark's asking for more trouble than plenty, and then some."

Kenny nodded his sage agreement. "Was I a praying man, I'd say Amen to that."

CHAPTER SIX

Point Them Out

"Aren't they back yet?" Disappointment tinged Thora's voice as she stood on the ranch house porch in the cold predawn light.

Out front, all was activity; Hobie and the Rocking H's temporary cook had been up some time and the rest of the trail drive crew had been turned out to get a hot meal. Dusty, with a plate loaded with ham and eggs, answered Thora's query, "Nope, but the crew have to be fed so we can make a start."

"A start?" Thora stared at her trail boss. "We can't start without Salt. Hobie can't handle the wagons *and* the cooking."

"Then he'd surely best learn, and fast." Dusty replied, "Tarbrush can handle the bed wagon today and, afore we need food, Salt'll likely be back."

"But what if they can't get the sourdough keg back?"

"Salt'll have to throw up another as fast as he can."

Mark came up carrying two plates; he handed one to Thora and they entered the house to sit down at the table. Ben Holland was already in the room and he greeted them. It never occurred to him that the Ysabel Kid and Kiowa might fail to get the keg back. He watched the worried lines on his wife's face and smiled, "You get fed, honey. There won't be another chance before night."

Thora sat down and started to eat. Through the window she watched the wranglers bringing the remuda in and realized something. "Tarbrush has been out all night. He can't drive the wagon all day."

"Reckon he'll just have to get used to it," Dusty replied as he started to eat his breakfast.

The meal was over and the two Texans pushed back their chairs. Dusty held out his hand to Ben. "See you down the trail, Cousin Ben."

After Dusty and Mark had left the room, Ben pulled Thora's head down and kissed her. "Now don't you get to worrying. You'll be all right, Dusty will get you through."

Dusty and Mark stood watching the other men as they collected their horses from the cable corral which had been set up, using four sticks as supports. The wranglers were having no trouble with the remuda due to the time taken the previous night.

Each cowhand came up carrying his rope and looking for one of his mounts to pass by. Then the hand brought his rope up with one quick twirl in front, then up toward the right and overhead, and sent the loop out to turn flat and drop over the head of the chosen horse. This throw, the "hooley-ann," was always used for catching horses in a corral. It was the best throw for the purpose, for the loop went right out, small and accurate, and dropped over the horse's head with the minimum of fuss. Using the "hooley-ann" throw, several men could all be roping at the same time without unduly exciting the rest of the remuda.

Dusty took his big paint for first horse. The stallion and Mark's blood-bay had come in separate from, but following, the remuda and ran to their masters without needing roping. Dusty saddled his horse and then, as Tarbrush rode by on his mule, yelled for him to take the bed wagon.

"How's the remuda?" Mark inquired.

"Handled wuss," the Negro replied cheerfully. "You all done got a big ole claybank that don't like us none at all."

Mark and Dusty could feel some sympathy for the Negro; both knew they wouldn't take to riding nighthawk. Tarbrush would spend the night riding herd on the remuda and try to get what sleep he could in the back of the bed wagon as it bounced along behind the herd.

Today he wouldn't even get that chance, unless Salt came back in time to let him.

Dusty swung into his low-horned, double-girthed Texas rig and sat watching Mark leading the hands out to the herd. Turning in his saddle, he saw Thora had one of her horses and was mounting it. The horse bounced a few bedsprings out of its system without giving her any trouble, and she rode to join him.

"Ready to go?" Dusty asked.

"Yes, as soon as you are. How do we do it?"

"Just get round them and point them in the right direction. I can show you better than tell it."

They rode after the crew, side by side. Thora gave Dusty a warning, "You'll have to expect a lot of questions from me. By the time I get back to Texas, I want to know all about trail drive work."

"You'll likely know," Dusty drawled. "But the first thing you have to learn is that we don't drive the cattle—or won't after we get them off their home range. After today all we'll have to do is keep them pointed the way we want them to go and let them amble along, grazing as they go. The hands'll only need to keep the herd moving, stop them from straying, keep strays from joining the herd. Keep the stock from getting too bunched, or too scattered. That's all there's to it."

Thora laughed; Dusty made it sound all too easy. She waited for him to tell her more, but they were in sight of the herd and there was no more time to waste on idle chatter.

The cattle were just beginning to stir from their night's rest and the trail hands sat their horses ready.

Thora watched Dusty. The small man halted his big paint and then took off his hat to wave it.

"Head 'em up!" he yelled. "Point 'em north."

At the order, all the hands started their horses toward the herd. Shrill yells came from the men as they urged their mounts toward the cattle. Steer after steer came up and started to move, milling and circling. Then a big red beast slammed through the others, horns swinging, and

bowling lesser creatures from the way. He was watched
with keen and knowing eyes. Mark and Billy Jack moved
in on either side of the big red steer and headed him
toward the north. This would be the lead steer, the others
would follow him, and, if he was able, he'd keep his
place all the way to Dodge.

The rest of the cattle were up as riders came at them.
They started to move and any attempt at going in another
direction was met by a fast-riding man with a swinging,
stinging rope. The swing men moved into position as the
cattle lined out, then the flank men dropped into place.
The drag riders for the day, cursing in the rising dust,
brought the rear up.

"Have to hold them bunched for a spell," Dusty told
Thora as he watched the herd start to move. "Cattle
aren't like humans—they don't cotton to leaving their
home section and seeing what's over the next hill."

To Thora, the scene below was one of confusion, but
it was orderly confusion. The cowhands rode fast, twisting and whirling their horses like the masters they were.

Dusty turned his horse and headed off, leaving Thora
watching. She rode toward the herd, wondering what
she should do to help and afraid to try anything that
made a nuisance of herself.

A steer broke from the line and cut off for the open
range. There was no hand near and Thora felt her horse
quiver. She shook the reins and allowed the trained cowhorse to get after the steer. Thora saw the horse knew
what to do and sat back to allow it to work. Heading
after the steer, her horse caught up alongside it, and then
cut round to turn it back toward the herd. Thora urged
the horse to a bit more speed. This was a mistake. She
came alongside the steer and a pair of long, sharp horns
lashed round at her.

Jerking her leg away from the lashing horn, Thora
lashed out with her quirt at the steer's nose, landing hard
on it. Bellowing, the big animal turned and headed back
for the safety of the herd.

Thora's first essay into cattle work had not gone unnoticed. The handsome young cowhand called Dude had
been on the point of cutting out to fetch the steer in and
had been an interested witness instead. He whirled his
cowhorse by with a yell of, "You'll make a hand,
ma'am."

Thora's face flushed red; she hadn't realized that she
was being watched. She turned the horse to head along
the line, and another broke out. Dude allowed it to go
and she brought it back again. "The next one's yours,"
she called.

Dude waved a cheerful hand; he had been told by the
trail boss to keep an eye on Thora, but could see that
he didn't need to. Thora was making a hand.

Dusty sat his paint and watched the herd moving.
From a distance, he had watched Thora start work and
was pleased with what he saw. Turning the paint, he
headed back toward the ranch where the remuda waited.

Lil Jackie watched the trail boss approach and licked
his lips nervously, waiting for his first orders. The horses
of the remuda were restless, milling in the cable corral
and waiting to be allowed to move out after the herd.

"Bring on the remuda, boy," Dusty ordered. "Let
them go easy and don't let them get out of hand. If they
do, and you can't hold them, light out for the herd as
fast as you can and get one of the hands to help you turn
them. Don't let them run into the drag; that could start
a stampede!"

Dusty stayed watching the remuda for long enough
to make sure his wrangler could handle the horses. Then
he rode to the two wagons. Hobie was seated on the box
of the chuck wagon, a bandage round his head but a
cheerful look on his face.

"You ready to roll?"

"Sure thing, Cap'n. Want for me to move out?"

"Nope, sit here until fall." Dusty watched some of
the Rocking H hands coiling the cable.

The two wagons started forward as soon as the cable

was inside the bed wagon. Tarbrush sat on the box of the second and relaxed; he was a fair judge of horseflesh, and also of mules. From all the signs, he could have gone to sleep and this team would follow the chuck wagon. That was the way they had been trained, the way Salt had them trained.

Dusty whirled the big paint and rode back toward the herd. He passed the remuda and gave Little Jackie a friendly wave. Then he was up with the drag men.

The hands were still holding the herd tightly bunched and hazing them along. This was only necessary on the first few miles; after that, they could allow the cattle to scatter more and let them feed as they moved. The odd steer still tried to break back out of the line, but the hands rode too fast for this to happen. Thora, her face smudged with dust, came alongside Dusty as he headed for the point. "How's it going?" she asked.

"Fair. We'll likely have a couple of head left when we reach Dodge."

They rode side by side until they reached the point where Mark and Billy Jack rode on either side of the big red steer. Mark turned as he heard the hooves.

"You fixing to run a trail count, Dusty?" Mark asked.

"Sure, soon as we get off the home range," Dusty agreed.

"Trail count?" Thora inquired.

"Sure, we want to know how many we've got along."

"Is that important—I mean, to know exactly how many we've got along with us?"

"Why sure, you know what they say about a trail boss?" Thora nodded in reply to Dusty's question and he went on, "I don't want you to think I haven't done the right things."

Thora smiled; it looked as if the Texans driving for her were starting to accept her as one of them. Looking back at the long line of moving cattle she remarked, "We're making good time, aren't we?"

"Sure," Mark agreed. "But we don't drive them this-ways again, not unless it's a real emergency. Likely make us fifteen miles today, then slow down to between ten and twelve. It won't hurt the cattle any to haze them like this today, they've been held down in the bottom-lands and are fat and sassy. They'll be leg weary tonight, ready to bed down."

"The ole red there looks like he'll make a lead steer, Mark," Dusty put in.

"Sure, happen he stays on top there won't be much trouble from the others."

Dusty pulled his horse off to one side, then sat back to watch the herd moving past. Thora joined him for there were a lot of questions she wanted to ask and this seemed like a good time to ask them. "Won't we lose time if we stop to count the cattle?"

"Would if we stopped. But, as we don't, we won't."

"Then how do you do it?"

"We'll show you, let you try your hand at it later." Dusty suddenly stiffened slightly and looked around the range.

"What is it?" Thora had seen the languor fall off Dusty before and knew it meant trouble in the air.

"Nothing. I just got the feeling we were being watched."

Thora looked around the rolling country; there was enough cover for any amount of watchers, but she could see nothing to disturb her. Neither could Dusty, but he had that instinct which came to men who rode dangerous trails.

They had covered three miles from the ranch by then and Dusty headed back along the line, making for the remuda. Others of the hands were taking a chance to go back and collect a fresh horse. Dusty watched the hands change mounts. Mark rode up afork the black which had caused the trouble at the rope corral. Halting Mark asked, "Any sign of Lon?"

"Not yet. What do you reckon to the herd?"

"Ben picked out good stock. Happen we get the sour-dough keg back we'll have most all we need."

"Why, sure." Dusty turned to scan the range again.

"You get the feeling we're being watched?"

"Had it myself," Mark admitted. "But I haven't seen anybody. When Lon gets here, you'd best have him light out and check."

"I'll do just that," Dusty agreed. "Bet you a dollar they get it back for us."

"Not me." Mark had the same faith in their dark comrade. "Happen he found him a pretty girl and stopped on to sing to her."

Dusty saw three riders top a distant rim and, even at that distance, recognized them. "Looks like her pappy done run him off with a shotgun."

"Sure." Mark would have liked to wait and hear the result of the Ysabel Kid's adventure, but he had work to do. "I'd best get back to the point."

Dusty headed back to meet the three riders. Passing the two wagons, he told them to halt. Salt was carrying the keg; Dusty could see that now, although he knew the three wouldn't have returned without it. He waited and speculated idly on how the recovery had been made.

"You took your time," he growled as the men rode up.

"For them few kind words of praise and encouragement, sir, we surely thank you," the Kid replied. "It makes us feel real good to know we was missed and wanted."

Kiowa grunted in sympathy and inquired as to their next duties. Salt held his keg and looked pleased with himself, but he didn't get a chance to speak.

"Take out for the rims ahead, Kiowa," Dusty ordered. "You fed?"

"Called in at the spread and took us a bait," the Kid answered. "Then come as fast as the oldster could make it."

"Oldster?" Salt bellowed. "Oldster! Why, you danged Injun, here's me done all the work and this is how I gets treated!"

"This's nothing on how Basin's going to treat you," Dusty warned. "He had to take a spare saddle after you lit out on his night horse, and he allows he's getting galled by it."

Salt headed for the chuckwagon and Hobie climbed down. He looked relieved when he saw the keg and, after taking care of the cowhorse, went to take over the bed wagon. Tarbrush stretched and ambled round to climb in the back of the wagon and try to get some sleep.

The Kid and Kiowa changed horses at the remuda, then rode back to where Dusty was waiting for them. Thora came back at a dead gallop and brought her horse to a halt beside Dusty's. She looked at the Kid as he came riding up and asked, "Did you get it?"

"No ma'am. Mr. Toon done killed all three of us."

"You smell like it!" Thora couldn't have said a better thing if she had tried. The Kid was treating her as an equal and a member of the crew. Thora felt pleased that she had been able to think of and get out an answer at him.

The Kid told roughly what had happened at Toon's spread. Thora got a far more accurate version later from Salt Ballew. The way the Kid told it, he had spent most of the night holding the horses, while Kiowa and Salt did all the work.

She nodded her approval when she heard that the trio had left Double T horses for the night herd and had not stampeded the herd. Toon might not be friendly, but he was a neighbor and had enough troubles without adding to them.

Dusty was also pleased with the way the affair had been handled; he knew there was far more to the story than his pard told. He also was pleased that the Double T herd had been left alone. Knowing the Ysabel Kid and Kiowa, he quite expected that when Mr. Toon went out to look for his herd he would be finding it scattered all over the range.

"Light back there and see if you find sign of anyone following us, Lon," Dusty ordered. "Kiowa, head out for the rims."

Thora watched the two men head off to obey their

orders, then asked: "Couldn't you have let them get some rest before you put them out to work?"

Dusty grinned; the young woman had a whole lot to learn about the trail herd work and about trail hands. They wouldn't miss the night's sleep and would be very lucky if they reached Dodge without missing more than the one night in their bedrolls. Tarbrush was different; he would be out every night riding the remuda, and so he had to try and get his sleep in the daytime.

The Kid rode the horse of his Comanche relay back, paralleling the line of the herd. He rode slowly and watched the ground, checking every bit of sign as he came to it. Once his sign-wise eyes saw where a coyote had chased a jack rabbit, in another place a couple of antelope had grazed their way along. He saw other signs, but none of them had been made by human or horse.

On reaching the rim where they first caught sight of the herd, the Kid halted and stood up in the stirrups to look around. The range was still and, apart from the dust of the herd, there was no sign of life. He rode across the churned-up, hoof-scarred trail of the herd and, at a distance of fifty or so yards, started to ride parallel to it, headed back toward the herd.

After covering about half a mile, the Kid came on proof that Dusty had been right. He found tracks of three horses where such tracks should not have been.

The Kid swung down and remembered just in time that he wasn't riding his big white. He held the reins of the Comanche war pony and bent to check the tracks. His first guess had been right; there were three horses here, but only one of them had been ridden.

The watcher had been up to no good, that was clear to the Kid in a few minutes of tracking. A man didn't keep to cover all the time if his intentions were honorable. This man stuck to every bit of cover he could find.

The watcher had stopped his horse, then turned and ridden off at a tangent. The Ysabel Kid could read the reason for that. From here the man would get his first view of Kiowa, Salt and himself, and he had pulled out rather than risk being caught.

Taking the trail and following it, the Kid rode slowly and cautiously along. He was as alert as the man who trained the war pony and no less savage. If he found the watcher, somebody was going to get badly hurt.

The tracks ended in a rocky-bottomed stream. The watcher was smart enough to figure that he might be followed, so had taken this simple but effective ruse to slow his trailer. It was no great trouble, though a long matter, to refind the tracks. The Ysabel Kid would be able to pick out the hoofmarks of the three horses among a hundred others. All he needed to do was ride in ever-increasing circles until he found the sign again.

That would take time, more time than the Kid could give at the moment—he had to report his findings to the trail boss.

Dusty heard the Kid's report and sat silent for a time, frowning as he tried to judge the implications. Like the Kid, he had all but forgotten the man with the three ghost cord-broken horses. There was no real reason to connect the two. Many men owned a three-horse string—or mount, as the Texans called it.

"Happen you or Kiowa'd best watch the back trail real careful for a spell, Lon. It might be the scout for a bunch of rustlers."

"Looks that ways. I don't figger on it being anyone from the Double T, they've had their belly full of us," the Kid replied. "Want for me to follow him all the way if he comes again?"

"Not if it'll keep you away from the herd for too long." Dusty turned his paint and they rode toward the point. "Take over from Mark for a spell while we make a trail count."

Thora joined them just in time to hear this. "You weren't joshing me about counting the herd?"

"Nope."

"But can they manage to count all these while the

herd keeps moving?"

Dusty watched the Kid heading for the point at a better speed and turned back to the woman with a grin. "They're surely going to try."

CHAPTER SEVEN

Trail Count

Thora watched the Texans riding toward the point of the herd. She followed and saw Mark and Billy Jack leave their places to ride ahead some two hundred yards, then halt facing each other about fifty yards apart. Turning, she looked back along the long, winding line of cattle and shook her head. It didn't seem possible that any man could count all the animals as they walked by.

Spurring her horse forward, Thora passed the herd and headed to where Mark now sat his horse, leg hooked round the saddle-horn and relaxed. In his hands was a long length of cord. Billy Jack sat hunched in his kak, looking, if possible, more miserable than usual. He too held a length of cord, the end trailing down.

Dusty turned and yelled, "Thin the line!"

The hands stopped crowding in on the herd. Slowly, the pace dropped and the cattle scattered until they were ambling along, grazing as they went. The trail crew still rode watchfully and were ready to handle any steer which showed a desire to head back to the Rocking H.

Watching the herd approach, Thora wondered if Dusty was having a joke at her expense. What she had seen so far of the trail boss made her doubt this. She waited to see if the count could be made with any degree of accuracy. One of the reasons she had wanted to come on this drive—one she hadn't mentioned to Dusty, Mark and the Kid—was that she meant to write a book about the trail drive work. She had written one book, about her first year on the ranch, and it was bringing in useful money for her. This second book should do even better, for she knew how little the Eastern folks really knew about the skill needed to trail a herd of cattle.

She watched Dusty and the Kid bring the lead steer through the gap between the counters. Mark pointed to the red steer and said, "One!"

Sitting his horse Mark continued to count and point as the cattle went by. At one hundred, he tied a quick knot in the cord, without taking his eyes from the herd, or losing count. Thora sat behind him, trying to make her own count; but she lost it and saw that trail-counting was far more skilled than she had imagined.

Mark counted on. At one thousand, he threw a loop instead of a knot in the cord and went on with his counting. He did not know that he was being watched and was oblivious of the fact that Thora had headed up the line again. All his attention was on the moving line of cattle. As segundo, Mark was eager for his count. It not only let him check how many head he was running, but also gave him a chance to see if any of the herd were lame, or showed signs of distress at the traveling.

The steers passed, each counted by Mark and Billy Jack as they went by. The segundo missed nothing; he picked out trouble-causers, nervous, sluggish cattle. In the early two thousands, he spotted a black steer with trouble in every inch of its body. There was a mean look about that steer, which meant that he needed watching or he'd stir up some bad trouble.

There were muleys in the herd, Mark noted. That was to be expected if not desired. A muley cow, one which had lost its horns, was not in any great favor on a trail drive. In fact a muley was always trouble. The hornless steer, among its horned brothers, was forced to the edge of the herd on the march and chased from its bedding place at night by any steer which felt ornery. If there were many muleys, they tended to bunch together for protection and baulk at the slightest excuse. Also the muleys tended to lose weight faster and feel the heat more than horned stock. Taken all in all, they were not what Mark wanted to see in his herd. One good thing about them was that they wouldn't last all that long.

Mark counted on, the swing men passed him, then the flank riders. The line of knots grew in the cord and the third loop was formed. Then the drag men, masked with their bandannas to keep the rising dust out of their nostrils, passed by. Mark could always feel sympathy for the drag riders. He had ridden on the drag himself and expected to do so again. Of all the duties of trail herding, the drag was the most onerous. The drag man rode in churned up dust, while the other hands were out in the fresh air. On some drives the drag men were poor-quality cowhands, who couldn't be trusted with any more exacting work. On this drive, there was no such disgrace. Every man, with the exception of Dusty, Mark, the Kid and Billy Jack, would take a turn at the drag.

The herd passed by. Mark totaled up his line of knots before turning his horse and heading along the line. On the other side of the herd, Billy Jack was also riding to make his report. Neither man took any notice of their friends' jeering comments on folks who had an easy life. The trail boss was waiting to hear the result of the count and a man didn't keep him waiting. Not twice anyway.

Dusty turned and saw the trail-counters coming and waved a man up from the swing. He rode out and waited with Thora by his side. She was waiting to hear how close the count came to the number Ben had told her was in the herd.

Mark was the first to arrive. He lifted his hat to Thora with exaggerated politeness, then said: "At an off-hand guess, I'd say three thousand, two hundred and thirteen."

Billy Jack cut around in front of the herd and came back to the trail boss. He could not have heard what Mark said, of that Thora was certain. Her smile died as he drawled, "Three thousand, two hundred and twelve."

Thora looked startled, her eyes taking in each un-smiling face. Dusty nodded in agreement with the count. Ben had told him there had been a tally of three thousand, two hundred and thirteen. The Rocking H crew had not been idle to keep the herd at the correct figure. Dusty had been expecting that there would have been a few strays, or even a few odd cattle which had sneaked in to join the herd.

"Bet you missed that dun muley in the eight hundreds," Mark told Billy Jack. "He went by with two big steers on each side of him."

"Saw him," Billy Jack answered mournfully. "Tell you where you went wrong. There was a zorilla in the two thousands; he busted back and got pushed in behind us. I bets you counted him twice."

Before Thora could ask the questions which welled into her head, the two men had returned to their places at the point. She turned her attention to Dusty. "Did they really count the herd?" she asked. "Or did you tell them the number just to have fun with me?"

"They did, and I didn't," Dusty answered. He knew that many of the things cowhands did and regarded as ordinary, appeared wonderful to the eyes of a greener.

"Could they count any number of cattle that way?"

"Why, sure."

"What was the biggest herd you ever saw counted?"

"Well, now," Dusty frowned as he thought back, "reckon it was six thousand, seven hundred and sixty-one head. The first roundup we made at home after the War. That was the first herd we brought in."

"Who counted it?"

"My cousin, Red Blaze."

"Alone?"

Dusty looked uncomfortable; he seemed to be blushing under his tan. "No, ma'am, I helped."

Kiowa came riding back at a fast gallop and halted his horse by Dusty's.

"Water ahead there, Cap'n," he growled. "Ain't but a lil bitty river, ain't but hardly swimming water."

"Good." Dusty was once more the self-assured trail boss. "We'll water the herd there, then push across. How about a bed ground?"

"Couple of good places over the other side. The Kid's headed out to make a pick."

Thora turned. She had not noticed that the Kid had

headed out as soon as he left the point. Even now she could see him crossing the river. "Ben and the hands always talked about the trouble they could run into when they had to cross water."

"Depends on the river. That one won't give us much trouble," Dusty replied, then turned his attention to Kiowa: "Take over the point, and tell Mark to come back here."

Mark rode back and joined Dusty. "River ahead, *amigo*," he remarked. "We'll be watering the herd there, I reckon."

"Can't think of a better place. We'll thin the line down a mite, then try and bring them in in bunches. Many muleys along?"

"Fifteen at most, fair average for a herd this size."

"What's wrong with muleys?" Thora asked. "I heard Ben and Sam talking about them. Sam said you might find them some use."

"They're trouble all the way," Mark replied. "See, cattle are some like humans. In every bunch there's a bully, and, being a bully, he likes to pick his man. That means the bully goes for a muley that can't fight back. When it happens at night, you get trouble. They stir the herd up and the night herd has work on. Get it happening on a stormy night and you can end up with a stampede. So, as soon as we can, we eat the muleys."

"Eat them?" Thora stared at the two young men.

"Sure." Mark pointed back to the chuck wagon. "Ole Salt isn't going to be able to head for town when he wants fresh meat, so he has to get it from the herd. He can either take good stock that'd likely get to Dodge and sell, or he can take him a muley that happen wouldn't make it anyway. 'Course that might not make sense to a real smart Yankee like you, but it surely does to a half-smart Texas boy like me."

Thora sniffed disdainfully. She realized that Mark was joshing her and felt pleased; it proved the men liked her.

"At least, we won the War," she pointed out.

"Sure," Dusty agreed. "By forging our money."

"Well, if you were only half-smart and let us, that was your fault."

Thora whirled her horse and headed along the line before either of the men could think of an answer to this jibe. Dusty whooped and slapped his big pard on the shoulder.

"That told us, *amigo,* Cousin Thora's making a hand."

"She's making a *Texan,*" Mark corrected, paying her the greatest compliment he could think of.

Dusty and Mark headed back to the point of the drive. They were watching the water and calculating its distance from them. There were other factors to be watched at the same time. The wind was blowing across the herd and there was little or no chance of their winding the water. With the cattle in the present condition, that wouldn't be too dangerous, but with a thirsty herd it was.

The hands were tense and alert now, more than at any other time. Every man watched his opposite number and also glanced ahead to see any signs Dusty might be giving. It was tricky business watering three thousand head of cattle. The herd first had to be moved just right, not too bunched or too scattered. When the leaders went down to water there must be no rush, or they would be pushed across before they drank their fill.

Dusty pulled out to one side of the herd and waved Thora to join him. They sat watching the hands working the herd. Thora could see from Dusty's relaxed gaze that all was as he wanted it.

"Uncle Charlie Goodnight always told me that the two most important things in trailing cattle are grazing and watering, and watering the most important of all."

Thora had not realized that Dusty was related to the old Texas trail drive master, Colonel Charles Goodnight, although she had heard of the old-timer. Almost everything that was known about trail driving was part of his findings.

Dusty had served his apprenticeship with Goodnight

in the early drives after the War. Three times, he had ridden with Goodnight, the first two as a hand, the last as segundo. It had been a hard school, but the finished product showed it had been well worth it.

Dusty watched the men headed back for the remuda to get fresh horses, and called to Dude: "Stay back with the remuda for a piece. See that the button can handle it."

Dude waved a cheerful agreement and headed on back to the remuda. Handling the horse herd was not the work for a skilled man, but Dude knew better than argue with his trail boss. He knew why Dusty wanted him back there. Little Jackie was fresh to this kind of work and might make a mistake. With a herd new to the trail, this could be dangerous. Little Jackie would get help today; from then on, he would be on his own.

Every man got himself a fresh horse from the remuda; they all knew that a fresh animal could mean all the difference in the highly exacting and very difficult task of watering three thousand, or more, head of half-wild Texas cattle.

The cattle were still moving along at an easy walk, but the hands came in to cut the first three hundred or so from the rest and move them toward the gentle banks of the stream. The herd couldn't just be allowed to come down with a rush, as the first cattle would be forced over before they could get their fill. Each separate bunch had to be brought in upstream of the last batch, so they all got clean water.

The lead steer and the rest of the first bunch were brought down and slowly allowed to get to the water. The riders waited until their cattle had drunk their fill, then moved them across. Even as the leaders started to swim, the water from above came down muddy as the second group were brought in.

Thora rode with the men, allowing her horse to work the cattle and doing her share. She came up behind one of the hands just as he cut loose with a string of Texas oaths hot enough to singe the hair of a bull buffalo. The hand stopped in midstride as he saw Thora was behind him; his face turned red and he headed his horse into the water again.

Thora realized that her presence might be an embarrassment to the men at such times. She knew that they cursed to relieve their feelings under the strain of working the cattle. To stop them cursing would not help their work any. She wondered how she could get around this problem and decided to ask Dusty to pass the word round that she——

A steer bellowed near at hand. She whirled round and saw the animal was down in the muddy water and floundering wildly. Jerking her rope from the horn, Thora headed into the water. She slipped out the noose and flipped it, from close range, over the head of the steer, then threw a quick dally round the saddlehorn. From then on the matter was taken out of her hands. The trained cowhorse she was riding turned and headed for dry land, hauling the steer behind him.

Thora watched the steer get to its feet on dry land and felt satisfied that she had helped it. The horse knew what to expect, which was more than she did. Bellowing, the steer was up; its head went down and it charged straight at its rescuer. Thora saw the long horns lashing up. Grabbing the saddlehorn, she hung on as her horse danced aside and slammed iron-shod hooves into the steer's ribs as it shot by.

Luckily for Thora her dally slipped and she saw her rope trailing off behind the steer, headed for the open range.

Dusty and Dude had witnessed everything and the trail boss shook his head to the hand's suggestion that he should go after the steer. "No need for that," Dusty remarked.

Thora went after the steer, caught it and turned it back toward the herd. Riding in close, she tried to get her rope free, but the steer avoided her. Her face flushed red with anger and she started in to call the errant animal everything she could lay tongue too. In her youth, as she had told Dusty, Thora had been raised in Army camps. Now the half-forgotten learnings of those early days poured from her lips.

Dude rode up and rescued her rope for her and, for the first time, she realized that several hands had been interested and amused listeners. They now were all regarding her with broad grins. Tossing her head back she made for the herd. One of the hands gave a wild yell and, whooping, the rest of the riders headed for the battle again. Without realizing it, Thora had passed yet another test.

From that day on, the men cursed the cattle freely, whether she was there or not. They treated her as an equal while riding the herd. In camp, none of them would have thought of using anything stronger than a damn, and would have tromped any stranger who spoke out of turn; but with the cattle, Thora was one of them. They cursed freely and without embarrassment. So did Thora.

The herd was watered and moved across the stream and Little Jackie brought his remuda down. Tarbrush was awake and helping; he had come out before the first of the herd were brought down and Dude returned to work the cattle.

Last across came the two wagons. Salt knew the herd would be bedded down very soon and decided that he would make his camp on the banks of the stream. He wanted to have a meal ready for the first pair of night herders when they returned. Salt had plenty of work to do; he had to prepare his camp and get the meal ready for the first men back. The hands had been in the saddle all day without food. If he was late in handing out the meal, Salt knew he would hear a few things about himself from the trail boss. He also guessed Captain Fog would do it real good.

Halting the wagon, Salt gave his orders to Hobie. They were to put the wagons in position to make a windbreak for the camp. Salt's two teams knew this as well as he did and moved into place without fuss. Salt climbed down from his wagon and nodded in approval.

The water would be clear soon and he would find plenty of dry wood to make a fire in the small *bosque* downstream. Near to hand were two trees which were far enough away from each other to be used as supports for a picket rope for the night horses.

"What now?" Hobie inquired as he climbed down to join his boss.

"Unhitch the teams, fix up the picket line, roust out the cable, start and collect me some firewood. Then, when I've got a fire going, you turn all the bedrolls out of the wagon. Then get some water. When you done that, I'll find you some work."

The herd had been formed again after crossing the river and were moving on; but now Mark and Billy Jack crowded in on the lead steer and slowed him down.

Dusty rode out ahead of the herd and the Ysabel Kid joined him to point out the bedground he had chosen. The Kid's judgment in such matters was sound and Dusty saw no objection to the open stretch a half-mile or so ahead. The ground was clear and there were no trees around; the cattle would settle down here with no trouble.

"Make a circle, Lon," Dusty ordered. "Kiowa's headed out the other way. Don't let him shoot you in the leg."

"Not me. I'm smart."

The Kid whirled his horse and was gone before Dusty could answer this modest claim.

Dusty watched the Kid fade into the distance and knew that his pard would find any signs of undesirable company. The Ysabel Kid was also quite capable of handling the said company with either his old Dragoon or his Winchester, if such handling proved to be necessary.

Turning, Dusty headed back for the herd and found that Mark was out on one flank, while Red Tolliver rode the point with Billy Jack. Mark sat his horse and watched the handling of the herd carefully. He had to ensure that the cattle were neither too bunched, nor too scattered, as they were brought towards the bedground.

Slowly, imperceptibly to a casual onlooker, the herd's pace dropped. The big red steer halted and behind him, the rest of the herd came to a stop. The hands started to ride in a circle around the cattle now, each man crooning out as he waited for the herd to settle down. Here and there a steer settled down on the ground and the others started to chew their cud.

Thora rode to join Dusty and Mark as they sat watching the hands circling the herd. Two hands rode from the herd, then made for the wagons by the stream.

"First night herd," Dusty remarked as he saw Thora watching them. "They're headed back to get their food."

"When do the rest of the hands get their food?"

"When the night herd comes back."

"Fair day's drive," Mark put in. "Allow we've made sixteen miles. But we won't make that distance again, not in one day."

"Nope," Dusty agreed, then pointed to the herd. "See that black steer; he's the trouble-causer Mark was talking about."

Thora watched the big black charge a muley and drive it from its bedding place. A passing hand eyed the black malevolently and snarled a curse at it. He halted his horse to wait for the cattle to settle down again, then resumed his riding.

"All right, black boy," Mark drawled softly as he watched the steer snorting and moving restlessly. "You keep on the way you're going, and ole Salt'll turn you into a stew come nightfall tomorrow."

The hands carried on their riding around the herd as the sun went down and the night herd came riding back. Then and only then did the men leave the herd and head back for the wagons and the food which awaited them.

Dusty warned the two night herders about the black steer and made a round of the herd with Thora, then headed for the flickering camp fire by the river.

Tarbrush was holding the remuda down by the river

and Mark had cut Thora a night horse ready. By the time she had changed her saddle, Thora felt hungry enough to eat the horse—Texas double-girthed rig and all. She left her night horse on the picket-line with the others and noticed that Dusty and Mark left their own horses standing away from the others, not even tied. The Ysabel Kid materialized as she was about to leave her horse; he had his big white and let the horse join the other two.

Mark pulled the chuck wagon tongue round until it lined on the North Star as Dusty and Thora came into camp. She watched and asked, "What's the idea of that?"

"What we call following the tongue," Mark replied. "Line the wagon tongue on the North Star at night, and that gives us our direction for the next day's travel."

The hands were all eating, and Dude looked up as the Kid went to the table. "Where you been all day, Kid?" he asked. "Ain't seen hide nor hair of you."

"Now that ain't right, Dude," Basin Jones objected. "You knows we saw him and Kiowa asleep under that bush."

"That's right," the Kid agreed. "That's where we're some smarter than cowhands. They ride herd, we sleep."

Thora went up; she had been warned not to try and eat her food off the bench at the back of the chuck wagon. This was the sole property of the cook and the privilege of eating off it was the highest compliment he could pay to any man. Not even the trail boss could eat from the bench; if he, or any man, tried, he got told to move in impolite terms.

The plate of stew Salt handed her looked very good and was almost thick enough to be cut with a knife. She barely noticed this as she mopped up the food with un-ladylike speed. There were grins from the hands as she handed up her plate for a second helping.

"Ben won't know you, eating thatways, when you gets back to home, ma'am," Red Tolliver remarked as the second plate disappeared. "Ain't but Lil Jackie cleared away his plate as fast as you."

"Yeah, and the language when that poor lil ole cow took off with her rope," another man put in. "It war fit to set a man to blushing."

"Evil associations," Thora replied. "I was never like this before I met you bunch."

The men finished their food and each dropped his plate into the bowl of water. Then each went to where the bedrolls were lieing in a pile and sorted his own out. They went back and chose their places round the fire, each man noticing who was on either side of him. This was the order they would sleep in all the way to Dodge. The men would need to know who were their neighbors. This was so that when they came in to relieve the night herd, they could get the right men without waking up the rest of the camp.

"I spread your roll for you in the bed wagon, ma'am."

Thora turned to find Hobie standing by her side. She dropped her plate and cup into the water bowl and went to the bed wagon. Inside, a lamp hung from the roof and she looked at her home until she got back to the Rocking H. There was some gear in the wagon, a couple of spare saddles, a keg of "good enoughs"—this was the name given to the assorted sizes of ready-made horseshoes which would be used in cases of emergency on the drive. The other gear consisted of oddments needed for the drive.

Near the gate of the wagon her bed was laid out ready for her. On the floor was a tarpaulin sheet which would serve instead of a mattress. On this were laid four blankets and three thick, quiltlike suggans. For a pillow, she had her warbag, which contained her spare clothing for the drive.

Thora sighed, there wouldn't be much comfort for her on this trip, that was certain. She sat down on the hard bed of the wagon, then moved on to her bed. On an impulse she lay back, to test how comfortable it was, deciding to have a few moments' rest before she joined the men round the fire.

Half an hour later, Salt came round the back of the wagon, climbed in and covered her with the suggans. Then he put out the light and left her to sleep until roll-out the following morning.

The trail crew unrolled their bedrolls now. Each man had much the same—two or three blankets and a couple of the thick suggans, with a warbag for his pillow.

Billy Jack had his bed made up and he watched Mark unroll his tarp. The big segundo spread the seven-by-eighteen tarpaulin sheet out on the ground. The tarp had snaphooks down one side and eyes on the other. In wet weather it would be wrapped around the blankets, and if the sleeper was on reasonably well-drained ground, he would sleep dry even in the rain.

Tonight was fine and Mark spread a blanket on the tarp, then lay the others ready to get into them. Billy Jack eyed the top suggan and remarked, "That's a right smart suggan you got there, Mark. Don't recollect you having it when we rode for Colonel Charlie."

Mark looked at the suggan with some pride. "No, I didn't."

Dude studied the material which had made up the suggan; it appeared to have been constructed from the remains of three gingham dresses, several highly colored satin frocks and some less nameable items of female apparel.

"Man'd say you've got a tolerable heap of lady friends—and some of them dressed a mite loud for ladies!"

"Got it up to Quiet Town while we were there," Mark explained to Dude as the other men moved in closer. "Miz Schulze and Roxie Delue done made it for me while they were getting over the fight in Bearcat Annie's."*

The trail drive hands had all heard of the great fight in Bearcat Annie's saloon in Quiet Town, Montana. Three townswomen had fought it out with the owner of

---

* Told in *Quiet Town,* by J. T. Edson.

the saloon and her girls to enable Dusty, Mark and the Kid to get into the saloon and take a gang of gunmen. From the look of the suggan it had been some fight.

The men yarned for a time about this and that, then rolled into the blankets. Dusty left the camp to check on the remuda and allow Tarbrush to come for a cup of coffee.

CHAPTER EIGHT

Mr. Allison Meets Captain Fog

The herd moved on steadily to the north, following the tongue. For the first few days, Thora was so stiff and sore that she could hardly bear to move. She gritted her teeth and clung in the saddle all the long days, collapsing into her bedroll at night. The hands watched her dogged courage with admiration, and every one of them felt relieved when she at last got over the stiffness.

Across the rolling Texas plain the herd moved, covering ten or so miles a day. They crossed the forks of the Brazos, the Prairiedog Fork of the Red, and carried on up the sparsely settled lands of the Texas Panhandle. The herd became broken in to the trail, and there was no trouble. The trail crew were a closely knit and compact team. There had been little or no trouble with the cattle, and Thora was getting to be a good hand.

Sometimes the herd would be visited by riders, either cowhands or ranch owners. All seemed to be surprised to see a herd so early in the season and most of them either knew or had heard of Ben. They stopped for a meal if they came in at night, also staying the night if they wished. All offered their best wishes and most were of the impression that the Rocking H crew would handle Kliddoe and Wyatt Earp both.

Thora was a source of interest to the visitors; she didn't know how her crew regarded her as a good luck charm and proudly pointed her out to the visitors as the best dang cownurse the West had ever seen.

One thing Thora noticed was that, although they were eating the muleys, the herd seemed to grow. Any unbranded stock they came across was added to it. Dusty insisted that all branded stock should be chased off as soon as it was located, but unbranded animals were held at the drag until they could have the Rocking H road brand run on them.

For fourteen days the weather held good and clear. Then they ran into rain. Not just rain, but torrential streams pouring down and flooding over the land. Thunder rolled and lightning flashed as the trail drive hands unstrapped and got into their yellow fish slickers and rode with their heads bent, hunched miserably in the saddle.

Dusty saw one man riding without his fish and headed back. It was Dude. The handsome young hand looked up as the trail boss appeared by his side and asked where his fish was.

"Like this, Cap'n," he replied. "I bought the damned thing new in Granite just afore we left. Toted it every day and near to got it torn yesterday when a steer hooked at me. So I left it behind today."

"That's asking for rain. Head back and get it."

Dude turned and headed for the bed wagon; he would never have gone without Dusty's permission and knew there were trail bosses who wouldn't have given it—not when it meant taking his place in line while he went.

Salt watched Dude ride up and told him in no uncertain manner just what he thought of a hand who left his fish in the wagon. Dude thanked him politely and rode to the bed wagon, where he collected his gear quietly to avoid disturbing the sleeping nighthawk. Dressed in dry clothing and wearing his fish, Dude headed back for his place by the herd.

Thora rode alongside the herd; she was uncomfortable and cold, but she kept to her place like the men. She wondered how much longer Dusty would keep moving in this rain. She found out fast enough.

For five more days it rained just about all the time. The herd was kept moving through the wet, soaking grass and fording rivers which were, to use the trail-drivers' term, over the willows. The crew used every ounce of their skill at each crossing and the losses to the herd were, by masterly handling, slight. The hands got what sleep they could, for there was no chance of finding some place dry to make a camp. Never were there less than four men with the herd, and two men always rode with the remuda. In the five days, Tarbrush and Little Jackie never seemed to be out of their saddles and even snatched a brief nap while riding.

There was only one consolation about this rain; it beat from the south and helped to keep the cattle headed north.

Throughout all this time, Salt worked wonders; every morning before the herd was moved on, he had a hot meal for the hands; and again, at night, there would be hot food when the men came in. Yet, for all of that, tempers frayed among the crew. The hands were touchy as teased rattlers and mean as starving grizzlies. Red-eyed from lack of sleep, dirty and unshaven, they rode, hard-eyed and silent.

It was at this time Thora saw more than ever what made a trail boss. Dusty was always there; he got less sleep than the other men and always seemed to be in his saddle. Now he was soft-spoken and diplomatic; then, when need be, he became hard, savage and dangerous.

The crew were round the fire on the fifth night of the rains, each man standing morosely, eating his food. Dusty watched them, sensing their mood and knowing that a spark could cause bad trouble.

Each man was gulping down his food, wolf savage and angry, wet and miserable. Little Jackie came from the side of the wagon, headed for the warmth of the fire Salt had made. The boy was cold, wet and more than half-blinded by the brim of his cheap woolsey hat falling down. He crashed full into Dude, spilling his food down the rider's new fish.

Dude roared in rage as his own plate of stew went down his fish front. The back of his hand lashed round, staggering Little Jackie backward into Red Tolliver.

"What the hell!" Red roared, pushing the wrangler aside and facing Dude, who was moving in, fists clenched.

Dude's face darkened with sudden anger, his hand dropped toward his hip. Red's hand fanned down and like the other man's, clutched his fish over the butt of his gun. With a roar of rage, he hurled himself at Dude. They met like two enraged bulls.

Dusty and Mark hurled forward to stop the fight, for in these conditions, such a thing could start a full-scale battle. Mark caught Red by the scruff of the neck and hurled him backward, then spun round to face Dude. But Dusty was there first.

"Cut it, Dude!" Dusty roared, catching the other's arm and spinning him round.

Dude snarled and swung a punch which had enough power to rip the top of Dusty's head off, had it landed. The punch ripped through empty air as Dusty ducked under it. The force of the blow put Dude off balance and Dusty's right slammed into his stomach. Dude doubled over and the other fist smashed up on to his chin. Dude looked like he was trying to go two ways at once. His feet shot from under him and he landed flat on his back in the mud.

Red Tolliver stood scowling at Mark, fists clenched and lifted. Then slowly he relaxed and a grin came to his face.

"All right, Mark. I ain't fighting you, 'cause I never fights nobody bigger'n me. That's 'cause I'm a noble, true-blue Texan. And 'cause I'm scared of getting licked."

The tension was broken then and the men were all grinning again. Billy Jack ambled over and looked at Dude, who lay with the rain dripping on his face.

"Ain't nothing like rain for cooling a feller's temper," he said mournfully, "and ole Dude, he sure looks cooled."

Dude sat up, shaking his head and holding his jaw,

then managed to get up. "Where at's the mule?" he growled. "Salt, I told you to keep them knobheads out of the camp."

"What mule?" Salt growled as he washed off the plates and refilled them with stew.

"The one that kicked me." Dude backed off hurriedly as Little Jackie carried the plate to him. "You keep clear of me, boy. I don't want no more spilled down me."

"If you feels that bad about it, pour one on me," Jackie answered. "It ain't wuth much more than that, anyways."

The tension was eased around the fire now. Dusty went to Dude and listened to Salt talking to the hand.

"I sure wish it was steak."

"Way my jaw feels, I don't," Dude replied, then went on hopefully: "You ain't got a steak have you?"

"Cook you an ole boot was you to ask real nice."

"Mean you ain't been doing that all along?" Dude turned his back and faced Dusty, before the irate cook could think up an answer. "Sorry if I hurt your hand, Cap'n. I don't know what you did to me, but you sure did it right."

"That's all right. Don't you forget your fish again—that was what started all this," Dusty answered.

The rest of the hands gathered around the fire and began to swap tall tales about the wettest time they had ever run across. They were still at it when the Kid returned with news that the weather appeared to be clearing.

The following morning the Kid's prophecy was proved correct. The sun came out and the crew were given a day to dry out their wet clothing before moving on once more.

The day they crossed the line into the Indian Nations, Kiowa came back with word that they were still being dogged by a man who was riding a horse and leading two more. The Kid had found sign that the man was still on their trail, but that he was keeping his distance. Dusty

refused to allow his scouts to take time out to hunt the
man down; he didn't want them too far away as they
were now coming into Indian country. However, he told
the Kid to take his string and make a circle to warn any
other drives that might be within three days' trail of them
to be on the lookout for the watcher.

Mark and Dusty discussed the watcher as they rode
at the point.

"Further we get from Texas, the better I like the idea
of him being a Kliddoe man," Mark drawled as he
scanned the range ahead.

"Sure. Had he been a rustler spy, we'd have known
before now. They wouldn't want us this far. It'd be like
Kliddoe to have a few men in Texas to dog the first herds
and point him to them."

"Happen you should let Lon and Kiowa go after him."

Dusty thought this over for a time, then heard a dis-
turbance from back along the line. He didn't take time
to answer Mark, but turned his horse and headed back
fast.

Thora was waiting, the black steer roped and snapped.
"He started to gore a muley," she said. "Reckon
he'll make us a dandy stew, or a couple of steaks."

Dusty laughed as he watched her lead the steer back
to the chuck wagon. Thora was acting like a seasoned
trail drive hand now. She left the steer in Salt's care and
headed along the line to take her place in the swing.

The herd was bedded down soon after, even though
there was more than half a day left for them to travel in.
Dusty was satisfied that the herd was ahead of any other.
He wanted to give the hands time to mend any damaged
gear and rest the remuda and herd.

The hands settled down around the cook fire, making
the most of their brief rest from the trail driving. Men
lounged around, talking. None of them took much notice
of the approaching buggy, nor of the man who rode by
the side of it.

"Hello, the wagon!" the man yelled.

"Come ahead, friend." Dusty gave the customary permission to ride up, without which no stranger would come into camp.

The buggy was driven by a thin, tired-looking and work-worn woman of indeterminate age. She had the look of a very poor squatter—the sort who ran maybe a hundred head of stock and tried to eke out a living with the calf crop.

The man was big, well dressed and powerful looking. He sat a big roan horse and looked arrogantly around. His right hand thrust back the lapel of his coat to show the marshal's star on his vest.

"The name's Garde, Town Marshal of Timbal. Who's herd is this?"

"Rocking H," Dusty, as trail boss, replied, "Miz Holland here's spread. I'm the trail boss."

Garde had known that without telling; known it as soon as he rode into the camp. He wondered why so small and insignificant a man could be holding down so important a position as trail boss. He looked round the camp, but he was no cattleman and cowhands were just cowhands to him. To a man who knew Texans in general, and cowhands in particular, the men at the fire would have told much. To Garde, they looked like any other such group, and he had never found much trouble in handling cowhands in his town.

"This here's Mrs. Crump," he growled, waving a hand to the woman. "She had all her stock run off, sixty head. Went a couple of nights back and, you being the only trail herd in the country, I reckon they might have got mixed in with your'n."

"So?" Dusty's tones were soft and silky.

"I want to cut your herd," Garde spoke to Thora, not Dusty.

"Certainly."

"No, ma'am!" Dusty spoke softly.

"What do you mean, Dusty?" Thora turned to her trail boss, but she felt nervous. That word, "ma'am" was there. She knew she had blundered badly somewhere.

"The herd doesn't get cut."

Thora knew that tone, too. It was hard, flat and it meant Dusty would brook no interference with his orders. She didn't know that every Texan regarded having his herd cut as an insult, and that any attempt was liable to end with gunplay. She also didn't know that Garde of Timbal wasn't highly thought of by Texans. The man was one of the kind of lawmen who never gave the cowhand a break. In his town, just to be a cowhand was likely to end a man in jail with a broken head.

The trail hands looked on, waiting for the outcome of this matter. Not one of them expected Dusty to allow any man to cut his herd. Much less when it was a loud-talking Yankee who boasted that he jailed Texans one-handed.

"The lady said I could," Garde pointed out, but he now knew who this small man was. He also knew that cutting the herd would be far harder than sneaking up behind a booze-blind cowhand to buffalo him with a pistol barrel.

"And I say you can't," Dusty replied, his voice, to Garde's ears, still soft and drawling. Dusty turned his attention to the woman. "We haven't seen your stock, ma'am. There's only our brand here."

There Garde had it laid out before him as plain as he could ask. He could now call the play in one of two ways: either he took Dusty's word, or he didn't. It was as easy as that.

Except that, if he didn't take Dusty's word, it meant he was calling the Texan a liar.

"There ain't another trail drive around." Garde spat the words out, wishing he had brought a posse with him.

"Not ahead there ain't."

None of the crew had noticed the silent arrival of the Ysabel Kid. He had returned shortly after Garde and been standing in the shade of the wagon, listening to all that was said.

"That means the herd'll still be round," Garde answered. "There war three men took them, and three ain't going to risk crossing the Injun Nations with sixty head."

"Said there warn't a drive ahead, mister," the Kid corrected. "I never mentioned behind. There's one back there, three days' drive behind us. I done talked to their scout, real nice feller called Smiler—mostly 'cause he never does." The Kid's words were mocking and got more so as he went on, savoring the shock he was going to give this loud-mouthed Yankee John Law. "Hoss he war riding carried a real cute brand. I read it to be CA."

"CA!" Garde's tones were husky as he breathed the letters out, "CA, but that's——"

"Yeah," the Kid interrupted, being highly pleased with the effect of his words. "The old Washita curly wolf, Mr. Clayton Allison—complete with Brother Jack 'n' Brother Ben."

The marshal of Timbal looked round the circle of tanned, unfriendly faces, reading pleasure at his dilemma in every one. It was one thing to ride into an unknown trail camp and try to look big. It was another matter entirely heading up and asking Mr. Clayton Allison, even without Brother Jack and Brother Ben, if he could cut the CA herd.

The old woman had been looking at the men around the fire. For the first time she spoke: "Them three ain't here. I reckon we'd best go and see the other herd."

Garde lost what little bluster he had left, all in one go. The name Clay Allison meant something to him and to every other Yankee lawman. Allison was a rich cattleman whose business in life was the running of his ranch in the Washita country. His hobby was the hunting out—and either treeing or killing—of Yankee lawmen. If there was one place in the West where no Yankee had best go and flash his fancy law badge, Clay Allison's trail camp was that place.

"Sorry, Mrs. Crump, but they're thirty mile off, right out of my bailiwick."

Dusty looked the man over in some disgust, and stepped from where he had lounged against the side of the wagon.

"You'd likely not have come here, had we been Allisons," he snapped, turning away. "Mark, get the herd moving again. Keep them going until night."

"Sure." Mark and every other man there had been expecting the order. With a herd behind, the Rocking H must be kept moving.

Garde scowled as he watched the men going into action. He wanted to make something of the stealing of the cattle and saw his chance going. His only reason for coming out here was to make a name for himself. The local election for the post of sheriff was approaching, and he needed the publicity to help him get the post.

Dusty watched the hands preparing to move out, then turned his attention back to the woman.

"Tell you what I'll do, ma'am. I'll head back to Clay's camp and we'll talk to him. If the men have brought the cattle to him, he'll give you them back again. Clay Allison never stole a thing in his life."

Mrs. Crump stared at the young Texan; she was a nester and never thought any cowhand would offer to help her. However, she could see no chance of getting help from Garde and agreed to let Dusty handle the matter for her.

It was dark when Dusty rode alongside the woman's buggy toward the flickering light of the CA fire. He called the usual greeting and the tall, well-dressed, handsome man with the black moustache and trim beard called for him to come and take something.

Dusty rode in, he helped the woman down and they came into the light of the fire. The small Texan looked round at the tanned, grim-faced group; he noted the two lean, handsome young men who were Clay Allison's brothers flanking Clay. His eyes went on taking in the lean, dark Indian scout and Allison's segundo, Smiler. The other men were all hard, tough-looking hands with the look of first-rate cattle hands about them. That figured, for Clay Allison only took on the best.

There had been much written and told of Clay Allison's wild drinking and his whisky-primed fun and games. Yet no man ever saw him drink when working his cattle; him or any of that tough, rough and handy crew who rode with him and would have died for him.

Allison looked Dusty over, noting the gunbelt which had been made by his own maker. He ignored the soft whisper that ran around the men about the fire. Even as Dusty accepted the proffered coffee cup from the cook, and introduced himself, the men were telling each other who he was.

"Trail boss for the Rocking H?" Allison remarked. "Thought I heard a buggy with you. How far behind are you?"

"Three days. But we aren't behind, we're ahead."

"The hell you say!" Jack Allison growled, "I thought we were the first up trail."

"Could still be," a medium-sized stocky man put in. "Hold him here and see how far they'd get without their trail boss."

"That's real smart, Smith," Clay scoffed. "You just up and try it. This here's Cap'n Fog all right, happen you reckon it isn't." He ignored the man again and turned back to Dusty. "Mind you, Cap'n, saw you one time in the war."

"The day we took the Yankee General, you brought the word where we could find him," Dusty agreed. "You didn't have the beard then, but I'd know you any place. Reason I came back to your herd was that some damned cow thieves ran off sixty head of stock and Garde from Timbal came to us. Reckons they'll be taken north with a herd. He got to crying and took on like to wet us out. So I said I'd come back here and ask you if anybody'd come and asked to trail with you."

"That so?" Clay flashed a look at the tough who had spoken before. "Now who'd you reckon'd be robbing them poor ole Injuns like that?"

"Injuns?" Dusty spat the word out. "You don't reckon I'd leave my herd and come back here for Injuns. It was an old nester woman and they took every head she owned."

Allison came to his feet, his mouth a hard, tight line in the light of the fire. "Is that right?"

He wasn't speaking to Dusty, but to the tough who had suggested holding up the Rocking H herd. The man and two more were on their feet, hands driving down toward the butts of their guns.

Dusty dropped his coffee cup and started his draw the instant after Clay Allison's move was made. The firelight glinted on the barrels of guns and the exploding powder rocked the silence of the night. Ahead of those of Allison and the other men, and before the falling cup hit the ground, Dusty's matched guns roared throwing lead into Smith and the man on his right. Clay Allison's gun roared out in echo to Dusty's. The third man hunched forward, then dropped.

For an instant there was silence as the men all watched the small Texan who had shaded their boss. There was no move until the cook stepped forward to pick up the fallen cup, wash it and refill it.

Allison holstered his gun and told some of his men to get the three bodies moved out of the camp. Then he turned to Dusty. "I never could stand a liar."

Dusty explained why he had come here and called the woman in from where he had left her. Clay Allison sat down again and told how Smith had brought the sixty head to his herd the previous day. Saying that they took the herd from the Indians, Smith offered to help work the CA herd to Dodge in exchange for safe conduct through the Indian Nations. There was nothing unusual in this arrangement; small ranchers often took on with larger drives on the same terms. Clay Allison was not even worried by the fact that the cattle had been stolen from Indians. He and most other western men regarded Indians as something to be killed off, and a man who robbed the Indians as something of a hero.

"Trouble now being that the sixty head's all mixed up with my own stock," he mused as the woman was seated by the fire. "I don't want to lose a day by cutting herd. So, if it's fair with you, I'll take the cattle north with me and sell them. Pay you for them now."

The woman agreed to this eagerly; it solved her problem of getting the stock to Dodge.

Dusty finished his coffee and waited until Clay Allison had finished dealing with the woman and had come back to sit by the fire.

"Kliddoe's ahead," Dusty remarked.

"Heard about it. You aiming to do something?"

"Happen."

Allison grinned wolfishly. "If you need any help, send word back and we'll come running."

"We'll do that."

"You've been having luck, or Ben did. We heard about his trouble and allowed to stop over to Granite and talk some sense to Thad Toon. Then we heard he'd gotten a crew and come on. Thought we'd be ahead of you. What you reckon Earp'll do when you hit Dodge?"

"You know Earp."

"Sure, full of wind and bull-water. Say, did you hear the word Bat Masterson passed about me?"

"I heard," Dusty agreed. "But I don't reckon Bat sent it—not unless it came to you direct."

"You've got a whole heap more faith in him than I have. You know him real good?"

"Met him a couple of times. Nice feller—fair with the cowhands. Waal, I allow it's long gone time for me to head back to the herd."

Ben Allison grinned and winked at his brothers. "Know something, Clay? Ole Smith had a real good idea, keeping Dusty here."

"What'd you have to say about that, Dusty?" Allison asked.

Dusty smiled, then he threw the cup into the air, shouting, "Lon!"

The flat bark of a rifle echoed the shout, and from the darkness came a spark of light. At the peak of its flight, the cup spun off course and landed, neatly holed, at Allison's feet.

Clay Allison roared with laughter at the startled faces.

"That's the Ysabel Kid out there, I reckon," he remarked. "Smiler said he'd talked with the Kid, but there warn't no mention of working for a drive."

"Lon's like that, modest. Reckon if your boys aren't going to hold me, I'll light out, Clay."

Allison rose and held out his hand. Dusty shook it, then said his good-byes and left the camp.

The Allison brothers watched the small figure disappear. Then Ben turned to Clay, "I never reckoned I'd see you licked to the draw, but I seed it tonight."

Clay Allison nodded, his face thoughtful. "I never allowed to see a man draw and use two guns as well as that either."

They listened to the sound of hooves fading into the night. Jack Allison laughed. "That Dusty Fog sure showed us how the game should be played. I nigh on jumped clear out of my skin when that rifle went off."

"Yeah." Clay Allison had not been annoyed, but amused, at Dusty's caution in leaving the Kid out there in the darkness. "Know something; he don't need any help to handle Kliddoe and Earp both."

CHAPTER NINE

Stampede

"What's wrong with the herd, Dusty?" Thora asked as she watched the cattle walking past her.

"Dry driving—and those." Dusty jerked his thumb toward two lean, grey shapes which flashed through the bush.

"What were they, coyote?"

"Wolf!" Dusty sounded grim. "They're hanging on to our flanks and waiting for a chance to pick up the stragglers."

A week had passed since the meeting with Clay Allison; and the Rocking H herd was now getting deep into the Indian Nations. The rains of the south did not appear to have hit this far north, for water was very scarce and the cattle had been on short rations for three days. The last day had been dry driving, so the cattle were disturbed both by lack of water and the lean, big wolves which clung to the flank of the herd.

The wolf pack, with the inborn cunning of their kind, realized the cowhands couldn't risk using guns; so they loped along the flanks of the herd, watching and waiting for a steer to drop out.

Thora watched the staggering cattle and the tired, hard-eyed men who rode by them. There was so little she could do to help them. She returned to her place on the flank, where she rode to relieve a man who was badly needed at the drag. It was the first time she had seen Dusty to speak to for two days. The trail boss was constantly on the move. At the point rode Kiowa and Billy Jack, for Mark was riding the drag. The Ysabel Kid rode a constant circle round the herd, hurling his horse at any wolf he saw and breaking the pack off, trying to scatter them without shooting.

The drag was now the key point of the drive. Mark rode there and had not left his place for two days. He was tireless in his work here, a veritable tower of strength. The other men had each taken a turn at the drag and been relieved; but Mark stayed here, tailing up the weakened steers.

It was hard and grueling work, riding in the dust-choked rear of the herd. Now and then a steer would go down stubbornly, waiting for death. When this happened, one of the drag riders would come in, lean out of the saddle, grip the animal by the tail and haul it back to its feet.

The weaker stock were all at the rear now and the drag men kept them going, trying to stop them dropping and pushing stronger stock out of the way of the weak ones.

Through all the dust and the lung-ache it caused, Mark worked on. He did the work of three men; every other hand who rode the drag tried to keep up with him but none could.

The Ysabel Kid rode to where Dusty sat his horse, watching the herd and trying to decide how he could ease the burden on the hands at the drag. The Kid brought news that was both good and dangerous. In one of his wolf-chasing circles he had seen, in the distance, the waters of the North Canadian river. The waters were not high just now, but they were still high enough to make trouble for the herd in its weakened state.

The biggest danger was that the herd might get scent of the water. If they once did——

Sending for Mark from the drag, Dusty held a quick conference.

"Canadian's ahead. Reckon you'd best take the point with Billy Jack. And send Kiowa to the drag."

"Sure," Mark agreed, "we'll have to hold that ole lead steer down until he can't but hobble. If the herd gets a smell of that water——"

"Yeah, we'll have us some real fun then. Happen we're lucky, they won't."

Mark looked back to where Little Jackie was bringing the remuda along, and beyond to where the two wagons moved at the rear. Tarbrush came from the bed wagon and joined the youngster. Mark turned back to Dusty and said, "We'd best get the remuda down there and watered before we bring the herd in."

"Why sure, the hands are going to need fresh horses when we try to hold the cattle in. Take the point, *amigo;* if we can't hold them, push them right across, then turn them at the other side. Don't let them start a merry-go-round in the water."

Mark knew this without being told; he knew that, although it was always desirable to get the herd milling round on land, if it ran in stampede, the same did not apply to when the cattle were in water. If the stock started to mill in the water they would close in and tighten. The loss through drowning would be terrible for there was little the hands could do to stop it.

"Only good thing is the sun'll be in their eyes," Mark pointed out. "That'll hold them from going in, but it'll give us hell when we want to get them across."

Dusty turned and left Mark to handle the point. The trail boss rode back along the line and to the remuda. Tarbrush and Little Jackie waited for their orders. Neither had managed to get much sleep in the past few days, but both managed a grin as Dusty rode up.

"Get the remuda up to the head of the drive," Dusty ordered. "The Canadian's ahead and I want the horses watered ready for the hands to make a change. Keep them well to the flank of the herd."

"Sure will, Cap'n." Like most of the crew, Lil Jackie used Dusty's Civil War rank when he gave them orders.

Tarbrush didn't take time to speak; he flashed Dusty a salute and kicked his heels to the sides of his mule, then started the remuda swinging around the flank of the cattle and headed for the water ahead.

Dusty turned and looked back at the two wagons,

which were ambling along behind the herd. Salt and Hobie each had a horse saddled ready and fastened to the side of the wagon. If they were needed to handle the cattle they would leave the two mule teams to follow and ride the horses into action. Salt had insisted the mules were watered, even at the expense of the hands. He had trained the mules well and, with them not being thirsty, could rely on them to follow the herd and not spook at all.

Just what started the trouble was never discovered. It may have been one of the wolf pack that cut in close without being seen. Perhaps the horses got either scent, or sight, of the water ahead. Whatever the cause, the result was the same. One minute the remuda was under full control, and moving at an easy half-gallop, the next they were running in full stampede and out of all control.

Dusty saw what happened. He whirled his horse and sent it racing after the remuda. Three of the cowhands came from the herd fast, all making for the remuda.

Then the cattle spooked and were off running.

"All hands and the cook!" Mark's bellow rang out over the noise of the cattle. *"Stampede!"*

Salt and Hobie piled from their wagons and afork their horses, to go after the herd. The two-mule teams never even showed any sign that they were alone; they just walked along, following the herd.

The ground shook as the rumble of three thousand sets of racing hooves churned up the dust. Every rider joined in the mad, wild race to get to the point and help get the herd milling round. Thora was caught in the rush and rode like a master through the whirling dust.

"Shout, Miss Thora, *shout*!" a voice roared out.

She let out a wild screaming shout and, faintly over the thunder of the hooves, heard men yelling. She yelled and shouted out until her throat ached and her voice cracked. On the other side of the herd, her opposite number yelled back and listened, while she yelled he knew she was all right.

Every hand hurled along the line, trying to get to the

point. This was no easy task, for a spooked Texas long-horn could run almost as fast as a good horse.

Dusty allowed his horse to run. Then, from the corner of his eye, he saw something that made him bring the cowhorse whirling round and headed at a tangent. He slammed the paint into Lil Jackie's horse knocking it staggering. The wrangler had drawn his gun. He lost it, then heard a roar of: "Don't ever try and shoot—you'll spook the herd worse."

At the opposite side of the herd, Dude was riding fast and well on his way, when his horse put a foot into a prairie-dog hole and went down. At the first sign of the fall, Dude kicked his feet free from the stirrups and lit down rolling. Coming up, he knew he was still not out of the woods and was in trouble—bad trouble. A Texas longhorn feared a man only so long as he was afork a horse. One on foot was easy game and ripe for stomping.

The steer lunged out of line, long, sharp horns swing-ing down to hook Dude from belly to brisket. The cow-hand grabbed for his gun but it had jolted loose and lay in the dust by his horse.

From out of the whirling dust a big blood bay stallion loomed, ridden by Mark Counter. Cutting in behind the steer, Mark leaned over, caught hold of its tail and heaved. The steer was thrown off balance and lit down hard. Dude felt a hand grip his collar and pull, then he was dumped across the back of Mark's horse. The steer got up, winded, and stood for a moment, shaking its head. Then it headed back into the rushing line.

Mark brought Dude clear of the herd and the cowhand yelled: "Let me down, Mark. Get after the herd."

Mark dropped Dude to the ground and hurled his blood bay back after the herd. Dude was clear of the cattle but still in trouble. From behind came the rapid patter of feet, and he whirled to see a wolf coming at him.

Dude saw his revolver and knew he had no chance of getting to it in time. The wolf left the ground in a leap and then gave an anguished howl and crashed to one side. Faintly Dude heard a rifle cracking and saw a scene he would remember to the day he died.

Riding his white stallion as if he was part of it came the Ysabel Kid, his rifle cracking at the wolves. At each shot, a wolf went rolling over on the ground. It was an exhibition of marksmanship which would have been hard to equal.

The wolf pack were cutting in, trying to get at the stragglers of the herd and at the mule teams pulling the wagons. The Kid came at them with his deadly rifle cracking. Now the herd were running, there was no reason for the Kid not to shoot. He cut down on every wolf he saw.

Dusty had dropped back behind the herd and seen Dude's trouble. He headed for the remuda and caught one of Dude's horses from that racing mass, then brought it back.

"All right, Dude?" he asked as he tossed its rope to the cowhand.

"Likely live, Cap'n."

"That being the case you'd best get afork that hoss and get back to work." Dusty looked at the lamed horse. "Can you get your saddle out?"

Dude walked to his horse and looked down; he removed the saddle. Picking up his gun he sighed, shook his head, then shot the horse. Saddling the mount Dusty had brought, Dude called: "Tell Mark and the Kid I'll happen buy them a drink in Dodge."

At the point Mark and the other hands had turned the leaders of the stampede. The idea was to make the cattle mill round, the leaders getting into the center of the herd and, like a coiled spring, get tighter and tighter until at last all movement ended. The dust died away and the hands sat their horses, looking round to see if anyone was missing.

Thora rode to where Dusty and Mark sat watching the herd. Her face was pale and she was gasping for breath.

"How bad is it?" she managed to get out.

"Twarn't nothing but a lil bitty stampede," Mark replied.

For once Mark wasn't belittling the matter. The stampede as such things go, hadn't been too bad. Mark had heard of stampedes where more than half the herd was lost. What he didn't say was that only the superb handling of the crew prevented it from being far worse. The cattle had run for almost a mile; but they had not scattered too badly and only the weaker members of the drag had been left behind.

Dude came up, hazing several of the weaker stock ahead of him. Despite his two narrow escapes, he was as cool and collected as ever. "Say, Mark. Next time you hauls me across your saddle, just watch how you does it. I've got ideas about how time should be spent in Dodge, and you ain't helped it none, if you follows me."

"I wouldn't, not less the wind was right," Mark growled. He could see the smile on Thora's face. "'Course, you had to be riding a company horse when you lost it."

"That's me, smart." Dude raised his hat to Thora and headed back to help collect the rest of the drag.

Dusty made a circle of the herd and surveyed the damage. Three steers had been killed and one more had to be shot. That was a small price to pay for what might have happened if the trail hands had been less quick off their marks.

The remuda had run to the river and were now watered. The hands took turns to collect fresh mounts and, when all were afork fresh horses, started to move the weaker stock down to the river and water them.

When the time came to move the cattle across, there was trouble. The steers balked and fought against being pushed into water when they could not see the other bank. Dusty sent the remuda across ahead, then drove the cattle in.

The hands closed in and helped the weaklings over, one man on each side of any steer that looked as if it might be in trouble. One steer went under in the swift water, but was hauled ashore on the end of a rope.

The rest of the herd was cut in groups of a hundred or so and brought down to the river, watered, then pushed over.

Salt managed to get his wagons over between two groups and started preparing the camp for the night.

The darkness was closing in when the last of the cattle were moved across the river and bedded down. Dusty was the last man, as always, to leave the herd.

The Ysabel Kid came over the river just as Dusty arrived. The scout was bloody and, across the rear of his saddle, were the skins of several wolves. He presented the pelts to Thora, who was sitting by the fire.

"They'll sell in Dodge, happen you get ole Salt to fix 'em."

"Thank you 'most to death," Salt answered dryly. "Whyn't you go out and shoot a couple or so buffler and maybe a silver-tip or two, me not having nothing better to do than cure hides for you?"

Thora stretched back; she was tired but didn't feel like going to bed just yet. "Well, if you've got nothing better to do, get on with them. The crew are fed and all you'll do until morning is stand in front of the fire and spin windies."

"I hired as cook, not as skinner for some danged Injun that goes round killing everything he sees," Salt objected. "Anyways," he was examining the skins as he spoke, "they ain't wuth a cuss, none of them."

"How'd a cook know that?" The Ysabel Kid walked off before Salt could answer this.

"Head-shot, every one of them," Salt grinned at Thora, "they'll sell for as much as the steers we lost."

Mark sat on his haunches and rolled a smoke. A black-sleeved arm reached over his shoulder and took it on completion. With a sigh of resignation, he rolled another, which Dusty accepted.

"Been a fair sort of day," the trail boss remarked.

"If there's any more cigarette-rustlers round here it'll be a worse night," Mark warned. "Don't you pair ever buy any?"

The Kid lit his smoke, then drawled. "I got thinking today."

"That's good, Dusty. We work and the Kid here thinks."

"I treats that remark with the contempt it deserves, Mr. Counter."

"Yeah, Mark," Dusty agreed. "First time Lon ever got round to thinking, so we'd best set back and listen to him."

The Ysabel Kid took this as permission to go ahead and expound. "More I think about it, the more I reckon that *hombre* with the three-hoss string is a Kliddoe scout."

"I'll give you that," Dusty agreed. "Seen any more of his sign?"

"Not for a spell now. I allow he cut round us and looked over the CA herd. Smiler allowed he'd seen sign of a man with a three-hoss relay. I make it this way: He followed us until he was real sure which crossing of the Canadian we'd make, then went back to look over any other herds that were coming. Soon as he saw the CA he headed back round us to tell his boss."

"Sure," Mark agreed. "Happen he knows cattlemen, he'd want to stop well clear of CA. I'd as soon have Kiowa or you catch me than Smiler, was I a Kliddoe man."

"Shucks, Smiler's of a sweet and loving nature, most times. But he sure acts Kaddo mean when he's riled. Which same he would be should he catch him a Kliddoe man."

"Know something?" Dusty looked at the other two, "I'd just about forgotten ole Kliddoe. What with the rains down south, then the dry driving up here. I reckon it's

time to remember him now. We're but three days at most
from the Kansas line. It's come time we found where
Kliddoe was at."

"Sure," Mark agreed. "And when we find his camp,
we'll cut in on him and make him think the hawgs have
jumped him."

"Happen we will," the Kid's voice was soft, yet the
other two had never heard it so latently dangerous sound-
ing since the day he faced the second of the men who
killed his father. "I've got something to show his Yankee
friends, that's so proud of their great and noble 'n' loyal
Federal hero. They'll likely be real pleased to hear it."

Dusty and Mark looked at their friend for a time. Both
remembered other occasions when he had let slip the
name of the Yankee hero, Kliddoe. Always the mentions
had been made with the same soft voice, the bitter twist
to the lips and that mean, savage, cold-eyed Comanche
look on his face.

"You'd best take out and find them come dawn,"
Dusty put in.

Before the Kid replied he came up, his hand twisting
back round the butt of his old Dragoon gun.

"Easy, Kid. It's us!" a voice yelled from the darkness.

Dude, Red Tolliver and the rest of the hands came
out of the darkness. In the firelight they all looked clean
and were now wearing clothes that weren't inch deep in
trail dust.

"Water's colder'n a blue norther," Dude remarked.
"But it surely beats trail dirt."

Dusty and Mark had been thinking the same thing
and they collected a change of clothes from their war-
bags. The Kid joined them and they all bathed in the
cold water of the North Canadian.

It was a far cleaner and shaved crowd who gathered
round the fire to drink and yarn. Thora went down after
the men had finished and, by the time she returned, only
Dusty, Mark and the Kid were awake, the rest all being
wrapped in their bedrolls. The three men came to their

feet with exaggerated politeness as she came up to the fire.

"Howdy, ma'am," Dusty began. "Where did—— Oh, it's you, Thora. I thought it was a lady, not seeing you a couple of inches deep in trail dust."

Thora sniffed disdainfully and went by with a jeer of: "If you worked, you'd get dusty too."

Dusty watched her climb into the bed wagon, then turned his attention to the others. Mark was spreading his bedroll down ready to get into it as soon as he had turned out the next night herd. Dusty shook his head and said: "I shouldn't have taken that bath until morning. Don't feel tired now. Reckon I'll head out and look over the herd. You pair turn in."

"Ain't tired now, myself," the Kid growled. "I reckon I'll take my mount and light out tonight. Got me a hunch that something's going to happen real soon."

Dusty had a whole lot of faith in his pard's hunches. They had a nasty habit of developing into full-blown, real come-up happenings. He told the Kid to light out, if that was how he felt, and not to get lost. Then he winded up with: "Happen you get to Dodge before we do. Tell that nice Mr. Earp we're powerful sorry, but we've just got to use his fair metropolis."

"I'll do just that," the Kid promised. "You roll my bed up for me, come morning. Ole Salt'll cuss me like to peel my hide if he has to do it for me."

Dusty watched his dark friend fade into the night, then heard Mark waking the relief night herd. The four hands rose cursing the drive, the cattle, the trail boss and the segundo.

Going out with the four men, Dusty talked with the old night herders. "They're settling down real quiet now, Cap'n," one remarked.

"Sure, happen they're all quieted down come dawn, we'll go back to a two-man herd come night again."

Crossing to the remuda, Dusty allowed Tarbrush to slip into camp for a cup of coffee, then returned himself.

The camp was all silent and Dusty built the fire up, then rolled himself into his bed and went to sleep.

Far to the north, the Ysabel Kid slid from the back of his big white stallion, removed the saddle and turned the horse loose. Picketing the Comanche relay near to hand, he settled down. Using the sky for a blanket and the ground for a mattress he was soon fast asleep.

CHAPTER TEN

Loncey Dalton Ysabel Rides Scout

The Ysabel Kid rode his big white stallion and led the three-horse Comanche relay tied in line one behind the other. The dark youngster was never more Indian than when he rode as he was now, on the scout for whatever he could find. He was very alert as he rode through the Indian Nation brush country, for here was a land ideal for ambush. It was from the shelter of the coulees and brush that the Kliddoe men would lay up, ready to swarm upon the unsuspecting Texas men who drove their herds along.

The land ahead held a curious fascination for the Kid. Not for him to ride blithely and unseeingly over a rim or into a coulee. He approached each with Indian caution and examined the ground ahead carefully. This alert caution was inborn to him and came naturally when in the country of an enemy. It was what kept a man alive on the blood-drenched banks of the Rio Grande country the Ysabel Kid had been born and raised in.

The big stallion stopped, snuffling softly and tossing back its head as it sniffed the breeze. In the same instant, the Ysabel Kid slid from the saddle, his Winchester joining him as he went into the shelter and cover offered by an old scrub oak. Except for one click, as he threw open the lever and slapped a shell into the breech of the rifle, there was no other sound or movement from him.

The white stallion knew what it had to do without telling. Turning, it trotted off back the way it came, leading the Comanche war relay after it.

Lying flat under the scrub oak, the Kid placed his ear to the ground and listened. At first, he could only hear the sound of his own four horses moving away; then, when the white found cover and that sound ended, faintly from the other direction could be heard two more horses approaching.

The Kid knew what was happening now. Nigger would have led the other three horses off into cover and was waiting for him to give his next orders. The white would not move until he whistled; then it would come back fast. The other two men, if it was two men, would be headed this way for the same reason he was following it. The way was the easiest; an old Indian war-trail, which allowed ease of travel with a fair amount of concealment.

Time dragged by and the Kid looked back to where, in the far distance, the dust of the trail herd rolled into the air. Then gave his full attention to whoever was coming this way.

Two men came into view. The Ysabel Kid's lips drew back in a savage grin as he recognized one as the man with whom he'd had words in Granite City, Texas. The other was a tall, lean, sullen-looking though handsome man, dressed like he was advertising a leather shop. He wore the rig of a cowhand dandy, this one, from his high-crowned, snow-white Stetson to the soft, expensive Levi's tucked into shining boots. Yet he didn't sit his big palomino gelding like a cowhand.

The two men were riding along, talking and showing such a complete lack of caution that the Kid thought they were slighting his abilities. He listened to their talk and was enlightened as to who they were. He also got proof that his guess about the watcher all the way north had been correct.

"Where at's this herd, Blount?" the dandy asked.

"There, under that dust. 'Bout a day's drive off and coming fast. They'll be all set up for the Colonel in two days. Then there's another herd behind them 'bout three days. Allison's CA, that one."

"That don't make us no never mind. Uncle Jethro'n me, we knows how to deal with them sort. We'll take us head-tax toll, or herd, from both of 'em."

Blount nodded in sycophantic agreement. "Sure, Cawther. We'll do us just that. The one I wants is that black-dressed 'breed——"

"Friend, you got your want!"

The Ysabel Kid left cover in a lithe bound that would have done credit to a buck Apache. He landed before the two men so fast and so quiet that they got the idea the ground had opened to sprout him, full-growed, Winchester rifle and all.

Both men brought their horses to a sliding, riding halt, hands stabbing at the butts of their guns. The dandy was the faster of the two, and he got first attention from the Kid's old rifle. The Winchester spat once, held hip-high, throwing two hundred grains of best quality B. Tyler Henry flat-nosed lead bullet through the dandy's shoulder.

Blount's gun was out. He jerked the horse's head round as the Kid fired a second shot. His own bullet missed the black-dressed youngster by inches as the Kid hurled himself to one side. The Kid's bullet was intended for Blount, but killed the horse instead.

Kicking his legs free as the horse went down, Blount swung his revolver in an attempt to line on the Kid. Loncey Dalton Ysabel didn't wait for such a move. He flipped open the lever of the rifle, flung out the empty case and replaced it with a loaded bullet. The Kid dropped while he was doing it and fired as he landed. Blount's bullet passed over the Kid's head, then Blount rocked over backward.

Cawther Kliddoe had slid off his horse and was trying to get his gun with his uninjured left hand. The Kid glided in like a Comanche headed for a white-eyed scalp-taking.

"Fool idea!" he warned and brought the metal-shod butt of the old Winchester round to smash against Kliddoe's jaw.

The dandy went over backward and lay still. Bending over, the Kid pulled the fancy, silver-mounted Navy Colt from the leather and was about to throw it away. Then he remembered that Little Jackie had lost his old gun on the stampede and was in need of a new weapon.

Looking down at the unconscious man, he said: "And you kin to ole Yellerdawg Kliddoe, you deserves to lose this gun."

With the gun tucked into his waistband, the Kid took stock of the situation his enterprise had brought about. When he came out from under the bush, he had possessed no set plan. A challenge had, unwittingly, been thrown at his head and he had replied to it. The net result of his impulsive appearance was one very tough, very dead spy, plus one wounded and unconscious nephew of Jethro Kliddoe, leader of the Kansas Border tax collectors.

The sound of hoofbeats brought the Kid whirling around in time to see Kliddoe's palomino headed back in the direction it had come and traveling at a fair speed. This did not enter into the Ysabel Kid's sense of the fitness of things at all. He knew that, throughout the West, a riderless horse coming home was a serious cause for alarm. The last thing he wanted was for Jethro Kliddoe to be given anxiety about the well-being of his favorite nephew.

One glance was enough to show that Kliddoe would not be going any place, and so the Kid was free to act. He gave a shrill whistle and the big white stallion came crashing toward him. Running forward, the Kid drew his bowie knife with his left hand and carried the rifle in his right. The Kid went up into the saddle like he was jumping a foot-high fence. The knife slashed, cutting loose the Comanche relay and, before the severed lead rope had fallen, the white was running.

The Kid sat his racing white and sheathed the knife, then booted the rifle. Next, he unstrapped and shook the kinks out of his rope while the white closed the distance with the running palomino. The chase was not prolonged; that palomino wasn't trying to get away and, even had it been, the gelding never breathed that could outrun that big white stallion, even when the latter was carrying its rider.

The Kid built up his noose and sent it flying out to drop over the head of the palomino. Bringing the two horses to a halt, he squinted ahead over the range. A rising column of smoke caught his eye, smoke where no smoke should be. The Kid made a careful note of its direction, then headed back to the scene of his encounter with the Kliddoe men.

The Comanche relay were grazing, and Kliddoe still lay where he had fallen. The Ysabel Kid hardly noticed them as he rode back, for he was very thoughtful. That smoke would most likely mark the camp site of the Kliddoe men. That was far more likely than it having been caused by a nester's cooking fire. The locating of the Kliddoe camp was now a certainty. Even without the smoke, there were tracks to be followed.

Swinging down from his horse, the Kid checked on how far away the herd was. He attended to his horse, then gave his attention to the wound in Kliddoe's shoulder. The young dandy was groaning his way toward consciousness, and the Kid talked as he worked.

"You never up and went and left me," he said to the groaning and uncomprehending man. "Now did you, friend. I'm real pleased that you didn't, 'cause you're our lil ole ace-in-the-hole. You're going to help take the pot for the ole Rocking H, less I miss my guess." He stopped and made a quick check around, then went on: "Ole Dusty's going to be real pleased to see you. Just think about that now, a Texas boy pleased to see you. I bet you never thought to hear that. Almost worth getting shot for, warn't it?"

Cawther Kliddoe had recovered enough to lay still and look up at the dark face while he listened to the soft, drawling Texas voice. He raised himself on his good elbow and spat out: "You'll get your'n! Wait and see!"

"Waiting long and lonesome and so are you."

"Uncle Jethro'll fix you and your bunch."

"Not him. Ole Yellerdawg don't want, nor like, no

war, happen the other side's ready and got guns. And, if he wants war, I reckon we can hand him some along of one real dead kinsman."

The full import of those words didn't hit Kliddoe for a few seconds for he was looking at a face as cold, emotionless and menacing as any Comanche Dog soldier. The face of a killer born and efficiently raised.

Spitting out curses, Kliddoe tried to boost his courage. The words died an uneasy death as a hair was plucked from his head and a bowie knife came into a dark hand. The Kid placed the edge of the knife to the hair and cut. Kliddoe had seen a barber do this same thing with a fresh honed razor, the result was the same, the hair split in two pieces.

"Hombre!" The Kid's voice cut in, mean and menacing as a silvertip coming out of its winter sleep. "You ain't got the brains of a Texan, the looks of a desert canary, but happen you got the sense of a seam squirrel. You get shut and stay shut. Rile me any more with your wicked words and vile accusations and I'll cut your tongue out. After what your uncle and his crowd did to my pard in the war, I'd as soon do it as not."

Cawther Kliddoe shut his mouth tight. He was remembering tales told of a handsome, innocent-looking youngster who rode a white stallion and handled a rifle like a master. They were not tales to hearten a prisoner of this man, rather they were tales liable to make such a prisoner wish he had been captured by raiding Comanche or Kiowa braves.

Time dragged by. The Kid lounged in the shade of the bush, watching and waiting for the herd to come up. Kliddoe managed to drag himself, first to the dead horse to get a drink, then to shade and lay back moaning and holding his shoulder.

Dusty rode ahead of the herd. He saw the horses and read from what he saw that his young friend the Ysabel Kid had found some trouble. He halted his paint and looked down at the wounded man. "Borrowing neighbor, Lon?" he inquired.

"Kin of ole Yellerdawg hisself," the Kid replied proudly. "And I called it right about that *hombre* with the three-hoss relay. You might as well have let me kill him down in Granite. I got round to doing it anyways."

"Sure." Dusty was long used to the callous way the Ysabel Kid showed when dealing with enemies. "You were right, for once. I'll write the folks to home and tell them you've finally been right." He turned his attention again to the wounded man. "Looks like some deck's gone shy its joker. Happen it's ole Kliddoe's stacked pile, he'd like to get you back alive."

"Yeah, he might at that." The Kid sounded doubtful. "He might like this *pelado*, but I can't see why."

"What Cousin Betty calls fascination of the horrible." Dusty passed over the suggestion that Kliddoe was, in border slang, a corpse robber. *Pelado*, in correct usage, meant a skinner of dead animals; but, used in the way the Kid spoke, it meant robber of the dead.

The Kid told what he had seen and what had happened since he met up with Kliddoe and Blount. "Allow I can find their camp now, was I to try real hard."

"Sure. But wait until after you've fed. You look all gut-shrunk and needing food."

They mounted the wounded man on to his horse and escorted him back to meet the herd. The trail hands were all too busy to take any notice of the three riders. The country through which they were now moving was thick enough to keep all hands busy. Thora saw the men and left her place on the drag. Her face paled under the tan and trail dirt as she saw the wounded man.

"What is it, Dusty?" she gasped.

"Not much. Happen you could call it old Yellerdawg Kliddoe's favorite nephew, come to call."

Cawther Kliddoe was staring at the trail-dirty young woman and hardly recognized her as the erstwhile belle of York, Pennsylvania. He grinned triumphantly, and sneered, "Howdy, Cousin Thora!"

Thora's stomach felt suddenly cold; she looked at the two Texas men, but could read nothing in either of their

faces. She wondered what they made of this greeting
from a man whom they hated.

Kliddoe grinned evilly at the cowhands. "Yeah. She's
my kin. What do you reckon about that?"

"I've got kin I wouldn't spit on, too." Dusty spoke
to Thora, not Kliddoe. He turned and waved to Salt
Ballew, who was coming up with his wagons. "Hold her
in a spell, Salt."

"You reckon being kin to Miz Thora'll buy you anything, *hombre?*" The Ysabel Kid's voice was soft and
deceptive.

"Sure, them hands won't take it kind to know they've
been working for my kin." Kliddoe leered triumphantly at the two Texans. "So, afore I tells them, you'd
best——"

The Kid jumped his big white forward, slamming into
the palomino. His hands shot out and dragged Kliddoe
from the saddle. They hit the ground with Kliddoe held
flat and the Kid kneeling astride him, knife in hand.
Gripping the other man's nose, the Kid held on until
Kliddoe opened his mouth. "You're going to have trouble telling without a tongue."

"Lon! No!" Thora screamed as the knife went toward
Kliddoe's mouth.

Dusty flung himself from his horse yelling: "Quit it,
you damned crazy Comanche."

The Kid slammed Kliddoe's head back against the
ground in disgust, then rose and sheathed his knife. He
turned and grinned sheepishly at Thora, his young face
innocent and almost babyish. She could hardly believe,
looking at that face, that its owner could be so deadly
and dangerous. She didn't doubt that without Dusty's
intervention Kliddoe wouldn't have had a tongue in his
mouth that moment.

"Sorry, Miz Thora." The Kid managed to sound con-
trite. "I forgot ole Dusty don't like the sight of blood."

Salt climbed down from the wagon; he didn't know
what was happening, who the wounded man was or why
the Kid had taken such drastic action. If he was surprised

at all it was only that the Kid had allowed himself to be swayed from his purpose and that the stranger still kept his tongue.

"What about him?" he asked.

"Throw him in the bed wagon, and see he don't get loose," Dusty replied. "Then I want some food for Lon."

Salt grabbed Kliddoe and hauled him erect, then pushed him toward the bed wagon. He did not know any more about the prisoner than before, but all he needed to know was that Dusty didn't want the man to get away.

Tarbrush woke up as the prisoner was pushed in. He yawned and sat up, scratching himself, looking at the white man who was dumped in. Kliddoe scowled and waited until Salt had gone back to his wagon, then growled: "Let me loose, nigger."

Tarbrush scowled. "I ain't heard that word since I took on with the herd," he said softly. "Why'd I let you all loose for?"

"Because I'm a Kliddoe, and we fought in the War to set you niggers free."

Tarbrush rolled his eyes. "You did now, did you? I'se been wanting to meet one of you. I never asked to be set free and, from what my ole pappy told me, I'd have been better if I wasn't free. He told me how them folks what had him treated him. He didn't have to ride no nighthawk for his food."

Kliddoe had an idea that the freeing of slaves hadn't met with this Negro's approval. "You get me loose, you black——!"

The words ended as Tarbrush folded a useful-looking fist and warned, "You stop all this here fussing, white boy. Cap'n Fog wouldn't want you to let loose. You jest get shet and let me sleep in peace or I'll beat you most ugly."

Kliddoe closed his mouth and sat in sullen, glowering silence as the Negro went back to sleep. The wagon lurched forward; Kliddoe twisted around to look out. He wasn't so tightly fastened that he couldn't get loose; then he could get out over the back of the wagon and escape.

The chuck wagon pulled in behind the other, instead of traveling in front. On the box sat Salt Ballew, his carbine across his knees and a desire to commit mayhem in his heart.

Thora and Dusty watched the Kid eating. For a time both were silent. Then she turned a pale face to his. "Dusty." Her voice was tremulous. "It's true about my being related to Jethro Kliddoe. I should have told you earlier but I hoped that we might get by without seeing him. I recognized Blount back in Granite and knew why he had come. He meant to blackmail me into taking him along. Then he could let Kliddoe know just where we were."

"I figgered you knew him."

"What will the men say about my being related to Kliddoe?"

"What should they say?" Dusty answered. "They hired to drive for the Rocking H, not your kin. Besides——" Dusty stopped, his face flushed red and his shoulders shook as he started to laugh. It was some seconds before he could stop enough to speak, "I'm kin of your'n too. That makes me——"

Then the Kid saw what Dusty was getting at and whooped in delight. "That means you're kin to ole Yellerdawg, Dusty. Just wait 'til I tell Mark about that."

Thora's mouth dropped open and she turned a startled face to meet Dusty's laughing gaze. Under the kin system of the Deep South, Kliddoe, through his relationship with her, was kin to Dusty Fog.

"We'd best tell the hands who we've got for kin tonight," Dusty suggested. "Likely, they'll all quit on us in disgust."

The Ysabel Kid finished his meal and rose. He went to the big white and vaulted into the saddle. The woman watched him go; she had come to know him pretty well by that time. There was no change of expression on his face, but she knew he was going to do something which pleased him.

Riding his Comanche relay and the big white, the

Ysabel Kid covered miles faster than a man on any one horse could have.

There was no trouble in following the two Kliddoe men's tracks, not to a trailer of the standard of the Ysabel Kid. The men had not tried to hide their trail, and it would have taken better than them to fool him.

The tracks curved away from the direction that smoke rose in, but the Kid took a chance and headed straight for the smoke. His guess paid off, for he came on the tracks of the two horses again on a gentle slope. The opposite side of the slope was where the smoke originated.

The Kid left his horses standing out of chance view and, rifle in hand, moved forward. He traveled across the ground like a scalp-hunting Indian, flitting from cover to cover, alert for anything that came his way. Although he watched for Kliddoe sentries, there were none out, and he wondered if he had guessed wrong.

Topping the rim cautiously, he knew that he had guessed right. From his place on the boulder- and tree-covered rim, he looked down on Jethro Kliddoe's camp. For a time, the Kid examined the land to see if he had missed any sentries. Then he decided that Kliddoe wouldn't bother with such things, not until his scouts brought news that the herd was near.

The camp was at the bottom of the valley, a line of small tents along a small stream. There was a large Sibley standing away from the rest, which would be Kliddoe's residence while here. The horses were picketed away from the camp, and a skilled man would have no trouble in getting by the Kliddoe sentries to let them loose. If the worst came to the worst, a stampede of the horses would set Kliddoe and his men afoot long enough to allow Rocking H and CA to get by safely.

From all the Kid could see, there appeared to be thirty or so men in the valley. Mostly, they had the look of poor farmers, not the usual type Kliddoe trailed with. Only five of the men around the main fire were of the hulking, dirty and untidy kind of scum Kliddoe used for his work. They would be all who were left after Shangai Pierce and his men hit the Kliddoe gang the previous year.

The other men would be new recruits and there were few repeating rifles evident among them. The Texans, with the exception of Salt, all had either a Winchester, Henry or Spencer that would give them a big edge if it came to war.

The Kid studied everything about the camp with disapproval. It would appear on the face of things that Kliddoe was slighting his ability as a scout. The "Colonel" should have been keeping his men out on guard, alert and watchful for the arrival of the Ysabel Kid. The failure to take these precautions was open invitation for Loncey Dalton Ysabel to do something about it.

Of course, Kliddoe's logic was easy to follow and to his Yankee mind quite right. He figured he had the Texans outnumbered and they didn't know the location of his camp, or where he would strike from.

It was good, sound reasoning, but it was only half right.

The Texans were outnumbered, but they knew where he could be found. Or would, happen a dark young man called Loncey Dalton Ysabel could ride his Comanche relay back and tell the news to his trail boss.

The flap of the Sibley lifted and the great man himself, Colonel Jethro Kliddoe, stepped out. He stood at the door, a fine figure in his Union Army uniform, complete with shiny close-top holster and the saber at the other side. He stepped forward to walk among the men and he was never to know how near to death he walked.

Up on the rim, a rifle came up and cold, red-hazel eyes fondly aligned the sights on the trim blue uniform. A finger closed lovingly on the hair trigger as the sights made a perfect picture over Kliddoe's heart.

Prudence held the finger. The Ysabel Kid knew he could shoot, kill Kliddoe and be long gone before pursuit could be organized. He also knew more would be lost than gained by dropping Kliddoe now. The men down in the valley would regard a murdered Kliddoe as a martyr, slain by the brutal unreconstructed rebels, and would paint for war. Besides there was an old, creased letter in the Kid's warbag to be fetched out and read to Jethro Kliddoe and his men before the great, noble and loyal Yankee hero died.

The letter was in the Kid's mind as he backed from the rim. It had been all of ten years since it came into his hands. For all that time he carried and treasured it, but he had never got near enough to Kliddoe to return it to the correct owner. That letter was going to come as a big surprise to a lot of folks; and Jethro Kliddoe wouldn't be the most surprised by it.

CHAPTER ELEVEN

Colonel Kliddoe Meets Kin

"Boys." Thora looked round the circle of tanned faces she now knew better than the men at the Rocking H. There was a hint of nervousness in her voice as she prepared to tell them her secret. "I haven't played square with you. When you took on, I told you we would have trouble with Kliddoe. I didn't say that I was related to Jethro Kliddoe."

If she expected the words to cause any great sensation among the men she was disappointed. Not one face changed expression or showed any great amazement at her words.

Red Tolliver was whittling a stick with the quiet concentration of a man doing a useless but enjoyable task. He tossed the stick into the fire and looked up. "Ma'am, I've got me a cousin who votes Republican, but I don't boast about it."

"Should think not," Billy Jack agreed. "You'd likely turn a man offen his food, talking about things like that."

"I got me an uncle who drinks sasparilly," Dude confessed, hanging his head in shame.

"Some place back to home I've got me a kinsman who goes to church," a tall, lean hand from the Big Bend country admitted sadly.

"What the boys are trying to say, Thora," Dusty finished for the men, "is they don't give a damn who your kin might be. I'm your kin, too, but they don't hold that against you."

"'Cepting when he turns us out for night herd," Dude remarked.

The Ysabel Kid looked up from eating. "Question now being what we does about said Colonel Kliddoe."

"Not knowing what you found out today, if anything," Dusty replied, "there're but three things we can do. Turn back to Texas, try to get round without him finding us, or pay."

"Pay?" Lil Jackie howled, disappointed that his hero should even consider such a thing.

"Sure, boy," the Kid replied. "Pay—with Colt coinage and Winchester bank drafts." He turned his attention to Thora and went on: "There's one thing I reckon you'd best know now, Miz Thora. Happen we meet up with Kliddoe, and I get half a chance, he's going to get hurt real bad. I had a pard in Mosby's regiment. Kliddoe caught him. He warn't but sixteen. Apaches couldn't have done wuss to a man than Kliddoe's bunch did to that boy."

Thora watched the dark, emotionless face, then she replied. "I probably hate Kliddoe even more than you, or any other man here. It was through Kliddoe that my father was disgraced and killed himself."

"How d'you mean, Miz Thora?" the Kid asked.

"My father was Colonel Langley Bosanquet. You may have heard of him?" she looked around the fire at the men.

There was silence for a time, then Dusty nodded. "The Quaker Wagons Massacre. We heard about it. Kliddoe wiped out five wagons of Quakers; allowed he thought they were some of our people."

"Sure," Mark agreed. "We heard, too. Ole Bushrod Sheldon was still yelling about it when I last saw him. Swore it showed what sort of folk the Yankees were. Never laid blame on your father; always swore it was Kliddoe who did it."

"The court martial didn't." Thora's tones were bitter. "My father was the senior officer and it was made out that Kliddoe was under his command. He swore on oath that father gave him orders to attack the wagons. My father's orders were for him to attack the Confederate troops wherever he found them. Kliddoe was a good friend of the Custer crowd and the Boy General stands by his friends. They had to lay the blame on someone, and my father didn't have many influential friends. So they broke him and dismissed him from the service. It broke his heart; he shot himself three days later."

"Don't reckon Yankees would have listened to much again' Kliddoe in the War," Billy Jack remarked.

"No more than a reb would have listened to the truth about Quantrell."

"Like to say that not all the South thought of Quantrell as a hero," Dusty interrupted. "Uncle Devil, my pappy and Colonel Mosby, always knew him for what he was. They led the group that outlawed him after Lawrence."

Thora accepted this, then went on: "I want to see Kliddoe face to face and ask him if he lied about the orders. I want to prove what kind of a man Kliddoe really is."

"Ma'am." The Kid spoke gently, yet his voice had the ring of truth. "Happen we're real lucky and Dusty comes up with something, you're going to get your proof."

Before Thora could question this statement, Dusty had moved into the center of the group. "All right, Lon. Tell it."

The Kid told it, with the aid of a bowie knife-drawn map in the soil. He told of all he had seen in his trip and finally sat back waiting to hear what Dusty made of things.

"Thirty of them; we were expecting fifty," Dusty mused.

"That's a tolerable handful, even for us Texans," Thora remarked.

"Sure." Dusty turned to Mark. "How many hands you allow you'll need to keep the herd moving? Counting Hobie and Lil Jackie?"

"Ten, twelve. In this brush we can't do it with less. With that few they'll have to move fast or we'll lose stock in this scrub country."

"Sure, but we can't stop, not with CA three days behind us."

"We'll handle it. You can't get round Kliddoe; he'll miss them two scouts and get more out. He can ride faster than we can move the herd," Mark drawled. "Go right ahead, we'll handle the herd for you."

Dusty had known Mark would say that. Now all that remained was to select his men and explain what he wanted. It was a good plan, if it could be worked.

If it *didn't* work, there would be stirring times round Kliddoe's camp real soon.

"I'm taking Kiowa, Billy Jack, Dude, Basin, Red and Frank. With Lon and me that should be enough. The rest of you, keep the herd moving. Ole Tarbrush's going to miss sleep again; he'll handle the remuda. Lil Jackie and Hobie'll ride the drag. This is how we play it."

Billy Jack lounged against the side of the bed wagon and watched the small rider who held the attention of every man there. He remembered other similar scenes in the war: A bald-faced youngster in captain's uniform standing in the center of a group of attentive men, planning some fresh attack against the union forces. Captain Dusty hadn't changed much since the days when he led the Texas Light Cavalry in raids that rivaled the best of John Singleton Mosby and Turner Ashby.

Thora sat back and watched the scene; it was one she never forgot. Often, on the long drive north, she wondered why these men, all bigger and many far stronger than Dusty, followed him and accepted his orders. Now she knew, knew from her own knowledge of great leaders. She had met Grant, Sheridan and even Lincoln; all had that same air Dusty possessed—the air of a born leader. It was that which had made Dusty a Cavalry Captain at seventeen. It was that which made him a trail boss.

"I would like to go along with you, Dusty," her voice sounded unnaturally loud to her.

"It'll be no place for a woman," Red Tolliver pointed out.

"Somebody told me the same thing about this drive. But I've managed so far and haven't been too much of a nuisance."

"You surely ain't!" Basin Jones agreed.

"You've made a hand, Thora," Dude whooped.

"Then I claim the right as a hand." Thora stood in the light of the fire, head thrown back and meeting the eyes of the men. "I claim it as much as the Ysabel Kid can claim it."

"I backs the claim," Billy Jack was on his feet, standing erect, hands hanging by the butts of the matched Colts. In the firelight, he was transformed. The miserable, hang-dog look had left him for once, showing what he really was—a bone-tough Texas fighting man. "Likewise I passes my word Miz Thora'll be safe."

"All we asks is that you stops back until we've got them hawg-tied." Dude spoke softly. "Then you can do most anything you likes with them."

Thora saw the pride in every face as they met her eyes. Never had she seen the hands of Rocking H look at her with so much respect. She smiled round the faces. The attacking party's worries at having her along were not that she would spoil things, but that she might get hurt.

"Right, talk's over," Dusty snapped. "Get the gear I want set up, Billy Jack. Use some of the boys to help you. Red, get out to the remuda and collect a couple of horses. I want to pull out in less than an hour. Lon, I'll let you take care of Cousin Cawther. Look after him real good."

Fifty minutes later the raiding party was mounted and ready for war. Dusty paused as the others rode out, held his hand out to Mark. "I'd like you along, *amigo*. Reckon the next drive we handle you'd best be the trail boss, you're missing all the fun."

"Sure." Mark crushed his pard's hand. "You just take care of the boss lady. And Lon."

The sun was just rising, flooding Kliddoe's camp with light when the great man himself stepped from his Sibley to look around the camp. The first of the trail drives might be within striking range that day, so he was already dressed in his uniform. He turned his attention to the picket line and saw his nephew's palomino wasn't there.

"Cawther not back yet?" he asked one of the men.

"Nope. Thought he'd be in last night, but him and Blount never showed."

The news didn't worry Kliddoe unduly; his two scouts might be making sure the herd didn't swing off at the last minute.

Looking round the camp, Kliddoe wondered how these new men would react to their task. The old crew had either gone under or scattered last year after the disastrous attempt to head-tax the herd of Shangai Pierce. The new men were of different stock from the savage crowd who had ridden with him in the War. Only five of these old hands remained; they were separate from the rest, for they couldn't get on with the new men.

Most of the new men had fought in the War, but they had fought in more conventional groups than his Raiders. They were poor squatters and only took on with him to make a stake for moving west. They might not like the idea of taking tax from the Rocking H herd, if they knew of his relationship with the owner. That was one of his worries; a couple of the men had served in Langley Bosanquet's regiment in the War and they might or might not recognize Thora. However, they all firmly believed he was appointed by the Governor of Kansas Territory to take head tax on the north-bound Texas herds, and so would believe they were acting in the right.

Suddenly a man jumped to his feet and pointed up the rim. The others all leaped up, grabbing for weapons.

Kliddoe spun round, following the gaze of the man. On top of the rim, sat three men on horses. The center one was Cawther Kliddoe, his arm in a sling. The other two were young Texas cowhands.

"Kliddoe!" the smaller of the Texans yelled. "Tell your men to lay down their weapons. Look up here and see what I mean."

Kliddoe and his men looked to where the Texan pointed, and all attempts to draw weapons ended. The top of the rim had several men, dark shapes hidden behind rocks or under scrub oaks. Each man was only in evidence by the shape of his hat and his rifle barrel which lined down on the camp.

A man at the rear of the group pulled his gun out. Then, from behind the camp, atop the other rim, a rifle cracked. Kliddoe and his men turned to see other men lining weapons down on them from behind. The man whose attempt to draw a weapon had brought the shot stood fast. The bullet had hit between his feet.

"Any more shooting, and poor lil ole Cawther gets his," the dark youngster on the big white called. He sat close to Cawther Kliddoe, yet the watchers could see something metallic glinting close to their wounded friend. "I've got him on the point of ole Annie Breen here. And she'll likely cut him in half, happen there's trouble."

"Do what they says, Uncle Jethro!" Cawther howled. "This here Ysabel Kid'll do for me, if you don't."

A man clawed at his belt, trying to get his revolver out. Dusty's right hand flipped and his long-barreled Army Colt cracked. For a fast-taken, off-hand shot at long range, the aim was good and lucky. The bullet sent dirt flying under the feet of the man.

"Hold it, all of you!" The Kid's yell cut across the distance as Kliddoe's men prepared to get into action. "Next to draw gets ole Cawther here cut in half. Then the boys on the rim'll down Jethro."

"Drop your guns, all of you!" Dusty barked out. "I'll give you the count of five. Then we start into shooting."

On the third of the count, Cawther Kliddoe screamed for the men to let fall their guns. He knew how large the raiding party was; but he also knew that he was number one mark for them. Jethro Kliddoe's men might fight off the Texans, but he wasn't going to be alive to see it.

Jethro Kliddoe was in an awkward spot. His men were waiting for his guidance, ready to follow whatever lead he gave them. With his old bunch, if he had been in no danger, he would have started shooting and let Cawther take his chance. With the old hands, that would have been their only thought. These new men were not of that sort. They wouldn't expect their leader to endanger the life of his favorite nephew.

There was another thought in Kliddoe's mind. He was under no delusion as to how the men of the South regarded him. Every Texas man on that rim would be lining his rifle, ready, willing and more than able to send lead into the hated Kliddoe.

With this in mind, Kliddoe took the only course left open to him. He stepped forward and removed the revolver from his holster to toss it into the dust.

"Move aside, Kliddoe. Let each of your men drop his guns, then get clear of them."

Kliddoe took the orders, and man after man dropped his weapons, then moved to one side. Every rider was disarmed and stood clear of the weapons before the next move was made. Four more riders came over the rim and the group rode down the slope. The sullen Kliddoe men watched the riders coming nearer, but none made a move.

Dude and Billy Jack rode forward to perform their part in the plan Dusty had made. They swung down from their horses and, taking a rope each, threaded the end through the trigger guards of the weapons, until all were fastened together in two piles.

A big, burly man stepped forward from the Tax Collector ranks. He hadn't the look of a Kliddoe tough, rather of a hard, professional noncom. "You can't get away with this. We've been appointed by the Governor to take tax on the trail herds. Colonel Kliddoe has a warrant to do it."

"You're wrong, Sergeant Marples."

The big man stared at Thora, as if he was seeing a ghost. Then he stepped forward and looked harder. "Miz Thora, by all that's holy! What're you doing here?"

"Taking my trail herd to Dodge."

"*Your* trail herd?" Marples twisted round to face Kliddoe. "Did you know whose herd it was?"

"He surely didn't," the Ysabel Kid sneered. "His scout never told him about trying to force Miz Thora to hire him down in Texas, and how he dogged us all the way north."

"Scout?" Marples turned his attention to the dark youngster who sat with a bowie knife resting against Cawther Kliddoe's belt. "What do you know about Blount? And where is he?"

"Gone, friend—to a far happier place than this. I surely hope it don't get too hot for him."

"You killed him?" Jethro Kliddoe asked.

"He ended that way."

"Hold it!" Dusty's bark cut across the angry mutter of the Kliddoe men. "You all reckon that Kliddoe is working for the Governor in this here head tax collecting?" The men growled their agreement. He went on: "That warrant is a fake. Stone Hart, of the Wedge, proved that once, and Shangai Pierce the second time. Kliddoe's got no more right to tax the trail herds than I have."

"You rebs would say that," Marples growled.

"Friend," the Kid's voice was that deceptive mild tone again, "you stand behind Kliddoe because he's a real, noble Yankee hero?" Marples nodded and tried to speak but the Kid went on. "Waal, I've got something to show you. Happen it'll make you real proud to know Colonel Jethro Kliddoe. If friend Billy Jack here'll tend to Cawther."

Kliddoe watched the thin, miserable-looking man take the knife and assume position as guard on his nephew. Then he stared at the thing the Ysabel Kid took from his saddle horn. He recognized the object and felt a sudden panic. If this dark boy possessed that thing, he must have something more—something that spelled finish for Jethro Kliddoe.

The Ysabel Kid dropped lightly from his saddle; in his hands he held a third model Colt Dragoon with an attachable canteen stock fitted to the butt. The gun was a finely engraved piece and, in the walnut of the stock, was a silver plate. All too well, Kliddoe knew what was engraved on it.

"This here Dragoon came into my hands in the War. Me'n my pappy were riding scout for Colonel Mosby and we got us a Yankee Captain. Pappy gave me this gun. The butt-plate reads: 'To Mason Haines, from his good friend, Jethro Kliddoe.'"

The Kliddoe men all looked at each other. Three or four of them, including Marples, knew who Haines had been.

"So that's what happened to Cap'n Haines?" the big man growled.

"Sure." The Kid didn't take his eyes from Kliddoe's. The dark young face was emotionless as he savored the moment he had waited for since the day he first came by the gun. "It wasn't the gun that got us all interested. It was a letter we found in the canteen that got us." Reaching into his vest pocket, the Kid removed an old, yellowed envelope. "Yeah, Kliddoe. I've still got the letter. Ole Devil kept me too busy to bring it to you afore this."

Kliddoe didn't move or speak. His face had lost all its color. The end was very near, if the men believed that letter.

"What does the letter say, Lon?" Thora asked, her face as pale as Kliddoe's.

"It's addressed to William Clarke Quantrell," the Kid replied. He ignored the sudden gasp from the listeners as he opened the envelope and took out the letter. "It reads: *'Will meet you outside Lawrence on the night of August twentieth. Am only bringing ten men as I am not sure how many more I can trust. Warn Anderson and Todd we are coming, as we will have to travel in uniform. Your information about the wagons was a dud. They were all Quakers, and not worth robbing. The only way I can avoid trouble is to lay the blame on Bosanquet.'*

The letter is signed 'Jethro Kliddoe,' and marked with his seal."

"That's a lie," Kliddoe began. "I never———"

Marples and another man moved forward. "Let's have a look at that letter."

The Kid passed over the letter without a word. Both men studied the broken, but still legible, seal on the back. Then they glanced at the writing. The second man took a paper from his pocket and compared the writing on it with that of the letter.

"That's Kliddoe's all right—and that's his seal!"

Marples spat in the dirt at Kliddoe's feet. "Yeah. And now I think about it, you was away from us when we heard about the attack on Lawrence."

Thora swayed in her saddle. The world seemed to be spinning round her. She could hardly believe her ears, but knew that her father's name was cleared by the letter that proved Kliddoe a traitor. More, it implicated him in the sacking of the town of Lawrence, Kansas, along with the gangs of Quantrell, Anderson and Todd.

Marples leaped forward to catch the girl and help her from her horse. "I never believed your father ordered that attack."

The other men turned on Kliddoe, their faces showing hatred. They stopped as Kliddoe's saber came out and made a flashing arc. "Get back, all of you!" he snarled. "I'd rather be killed by these rebel scum than by you. Go ahead, shoot me down. There's not one of you would dare face me with a saber."

"Well now, I wouldn't say that."

The soft-spoken words cut across the shouting of the crowd and stilled it as they turned to see who had spoken.

Kliddoe studied the small man on the big paint stallion. "Who might you be?"

"The name is Dusty Fog, Captain. Texas Light Cavalry. Is there another saber in the camp?"

"There is, in my Sibley." For a moment, there was a gleam in Kliddoe's eyes.

"Get it, Lon," Dusty ordered. "Dude, take this gent here and collect Kliddoe's horse. Let the gent saddle it and fetch it back."

Marples and the Texan walked away toward the horse-lines to pick Kliddoe's mount. Dude was relaxed and showed no suspicion that any foul play might be contemplated by Marples, and the northern man ignored the gun in the Texan's holster.

The Kid crossed to the Sibley to collect the saber. He had wanted to settle with Kliddoe himself, but Dusty had taken the play from him by accepting the challenge. He promised himself that he would sit out as long as Kliddoe played fair; but at the first sign of treachery, he would be free to take whatever hand he felt was required in the matter.

Thora came to Dusty, who smiled down at her worried face. "Dusty, you mustn't go through with this. Kliddoe is good with a saber."

"He called us rebel scum." Dusty's eyes were cold. "No man can call me that and live."

The Kliddoe men were talking among themselves. The original five moved away from the rest watching the two piles of guns on the ground. One of the other men stepped forward to address Dusty: "Cap'n Fog, we all know you by reputation. You fought as a soldier in the War and behaved with honor. We don't see any need for you to go through with this and, if you'll let us, we'll take Kliddoe in for trial."

"Thank you, sir. But this is between Kliddoe and me. He called the play, so we'll let them fall and see how they lie."

The Ysabel Kid returned to hand over the saber to Dusty. He looked around, then glanced at Cawther Kliddoe, "Didn't you tell these gents how many men were up on the rim?"

CHAPTER TWELVE

Captain Fog Shows More Talent

At the Kid's words every man looked up toward the rim. The figures with the rifles were still there, alert and motionless. Motionless. Every Kliddoe man looked harder; slowly it came to them. There was only one man on each side of the rim. The rest of the attacking force were nothing but dummies, hats stuck on bedrolls. In the half light of the dawn, with the rifles sticking out, they had been enough to fool Kliddoe and his men.

For a moment there was silence. Then Marples threw back his head and roared with laughter. Man after man of the new Kliddoe men joined in the laughter, slapping each other on the back in their delight at the neat way they had been tricked.

"You danged rebs!" Marples gasped at last. "You're trickier than a city three-card monte man."

Kliddoe removed his belt, then stripped off his coat and rolled up his sleeves. He felt admiration for this small, soft-talking Texas man who had fooled him. Taking the saber, he walked to his horse. He was in bad trouble and likely would die one way or the other. His one wish was to kill the man who had outwitted and ended him.

Dusty unbuckled his gunbelt and handed it to Marples in silent tribute to the man's honesty. Then he checked the girths of the saddle, patted the neck of the big paint and swung up. Kliddoe watched Dusty, a secretive sneer playing round his lips. He rode out into the open away from the camp. The Texan followed. They halted, facing each other, some thirty yards apart. Kliddoe lifted his saber in a mocking salute and noted that the Texan at least knew how to hold and salute with a saber.

Lounging easily in the saddle, Dusty hefted the long saber. It was sharp enough and balanced well, but he would have preferred to be using his own Confederate, Haiman-made saber for a serious fight.

Billy Jack stepped forward and asked formally: "Are you ready, Colonel Kliddoe?" Kliddoe nodded. "Captain Fog?" Dusty agreed. "Then fight!"

The two horses leapt forward as Billy Jack's words cracked out. Kliddoe sat erect in his saddle, saber held at the guard, ready for use. In contrast, Dusty appeared to be lounging in his kak, his saber loosely pointing along the neck of his horse. It was plain that he was the better horseman of the two and, in an affair of this kind, the better rider had an edge.

Kliddoe hurled his big black horse full at Dusty's mount, trying to knock the paint off its feet. Too late, he realized just how big the stallion was. At the last moment, he tried to swing the black clear, but Dusty slammed his paint into it and staggered it. Kliddoe brought round his saber in a backhand slash at the Texan's head. Dusty parried the cut, deflected it, then flickered out the point in a thrust. It was Kliddoe's turn to parry now; he caught the blade and turned it just in time, then spurred his horse past. Dusty cut at Kliddoe and almost scored a hit as the other man rode clear.

The paint was as fast on its feet as many cutting horses and came round before Kliddoe got his black round. They came together, the Yankee rising in his stirrups to get more strength behind each blow and to take advantage of his extra reach. He was revising his opinion of the fighting qualities of his opponent. At first, he had thought Dusty had the basic rudiments of the saber. Now he knew different; the Texan was very good.

Dusty for his part, was alert, watching every move and thanking the providence which had caused him to keep up his saber-practice down in the Rio Hondo country. Steering the paint by knee pressure alone, Dusty used the point of his weapon in flickering thrusts. He knew he had to tire the other man. Kliddoe fought savagely, his saber cutting and slashing; but all the time, that flickering point kept him back and gave him trouble.

They separated and rode in a circle, the paint turning the faster. Kliddoe hauled back on the mouth of his horse, making it rear high, hooves lashing down at Dusty. The Texan slid over the flank of his paint, out of the saddle even as the hooves hit his saddle. Then the paint was past the black. Dusty was still holding the saddle horn with his left hand. He bounded lightly and went afork with a leap. Bringing the paint round, he headed back at Kliddoe.

The blades licked and glinted in the early morning sun. Kliddoe was still trying to get an advantage from his extra reach, but Dusty's fast-moving point was something he couldn't get by. The watchers studied the fight; some of them knew saber work and could see that both men were even in skill. Only the Texan's superior riding was tilting the balance. However, Dusty knew that his paint was tiring. The big horse had been worked hard against the grain-fed freshness of Kliddoe's black.

With this in mind, Dusty started to attack himself, forcing the paint in, point licking at Kliddoe with a speed and precision that drove the bigger man back.

Desperately, Kliddoe beat at the saber. Then, with his left hand, he forced Dusty's blade down on to his saddle. Raising the hilt of his weapon, he smashed it down on the blade. A moan went up from the crowd as Dusty's saber smashed, the broken blade falling to the ground.

Kliddoe screamed in triumph and he slashed at the Texan. His blade was parried by the broken stub of blade, then Dusty was by him and clear.

Hauling on the reins, Kliddoe brought his horse round, tearing at its mouth. Dusty rode clear, but even now was bringing the paint round again. He threw the broken saber to one side, then sent the paint at Kliddoe. The other man rode forward, guessing what Dusty would try. The Texan was going to swing by on the left, to avoid a saber cut, and hang over the side of his saddle. Rising in his stirrups, Kliddoe twisted himself slightly, ready to cut at the leg as the Texan went by him.

Nearer the two horses came, hooves thundering and dirt flying as they closed on each other. Kliddoe saw the Texan was looking to his left and prepared to cut down, severing Dusty's leg, if he rode Indian style over the flank.

At the last moment Dusty's paint swung. Kliddoe gave a startled curse; the horse was going to his right. He tried to turn back, felt a pair of hands grip his leg and haul his foot from the stirrup. Then he was falling from his horse, landing hard, but he still held his saber as he came up.

Dusty came from his saddle before the paint halted. He landed lightly, turning to face Kliddoe. The other men started to run forward to stop this unfair fight. Kliddoe saw this and rushed in. He swung wildly and Dusty avoided the blow. Throwing the saber aside, Kliddoe made his supreme bid. The little derringer he had hidden in his waistband came out, lined.

Coming into the attack Dusty saw that he was too late; the murderous single-shot weapon came up to line on him. A shot roared and Kliddoe staggered forward as lead hit him. An instant later the Ysabel Kid's bowie knife sank in between his shoulder-blades.

Marples hefted Dusty's Colt, then said apologetically: "I'm sorry, Cap'n Fog. Didn't figger you can lick a hideout gun with your bare hands, so I cut in."

The men swarmed forward eagerly. One stopped and collected the two parts of the broken saber. Examining the blade, he spat out a curse: "Some hero—the blade of the saber's been weakened."

The broken saber was passed from hand to hand. Man after man saw the telltale marks where the blade had been weakened in forging. It was an old trick of professional dualists. Both blades were the same. They would hold up under normal fighting, but a sharp blow at the right spot snapped the steel.

"And we reckoned he was some feller!" a man growled.

The five old Kliddoe men and Cawther were ignored during the fight. They saw their chance now and dashed for the piles of weapons. One cut the rope and threw guns out to the others. From up the slope a rifle cracked; Cawther Kliddoe went down as he clawed up a revolver.

The crowd saw what had happened and scattered. The five Kliddoe toughs had their guns. These were firing at their erstwhile comrades, even as the Texans got into action. Billy Jack was the first man started, his right-hand gun throwing lead an instant ahead of Dude's. Then the other men joined in. Three of the Kliddoe men went down in the first roaring Texas volley. The fourth crumpled up to a fast-thrown shot by Marples and the fifth sent Billy Jack's hat flying from his head. Just who got this last man was never discovered. There were five holes in him, when the men checked. Any one of these would have been fatal.

Stepping forward, Marples handed Dusty his gunbelt. "Cap'n Fog, sir, there's been a lot of foolishness done by men like Kliddoe since the War. He kept us thinking that we were still fighting you rebs. I reckon it was for his own profit, same as he fought in the War. I'll give you my word that there'll be no more head-taxing done on the border."

Dusty buckled on his gunbelt again, then held out his hand to Marples. "That'll be all right with us. Kliddoe and his old bunch have all gone under, I reckon you can tend to them. We'd best get back to the herd."

"Joe, walk the Cap'n's paint until it cools," Marples snapped. "Bill, you saddle a hoss for him to ride back to his herd." Turning to the Kid, he took the old letter from his pocket. "I'd like to keep this. I aim to see that Colonel Bosanquet's name is cleared."

"You'll have trouble, friend," the Kid answered. "Custer and his bunch won't want it showing one of their friends played both sides."

"I'll do it," Marples promised, his voice grim. "I

know a few folks who'd be willing to help. One of the Colonel's friends is our Senator—he'll see the truth is known."

There were tears in Thora's eyes as she shook hands with the big ex-sergeant. She knew that he would try and clear her father's name. "I don't care if they don't clear him publicly," she said, "as long as our friends know father didn't order that attack."

The Kid looked at the letter, a half-smile on his lips. "You take good care of it, friend. I have all these years."

"You coming, Miz Thora?" Billy Jack asked.

"Reckon so." She turned her horse and followed.

Billy Jack turned to Dusty. "You nigh on skeered me to death, Cap'n. Back there, when that saber got bust. 'Course I knowed you could handle him."

"That why you near to poked my eye out with that ole Colt?" Dude asked. "Trying to line on Kliddoe."

"Warn't doing no such thing. I was just trying to see that my sights was on straight. Anyways, you'n' Basin near to beat my head in waving your guns round."

"Sure. We was thinking our sights warn't too straight neither," Basin drawled. "Taken all in all, I reckon we done a good day's work."

The horses were headed at a good pace, making for where the dust cloud marked their herd.

"I never thought I'd see the day when I'd be pleased to know you three fellers," Thora remarked. "It was a lucky day when you came along. I'd almost made my mind up to tell you we didn't need any men, back in Granite. I thought you looked too young to ride a herd. I'm pleased that you took on. I can't believe that my father's name is cleared. It's hard to believe the Kid would keep that letter all this time."

"Lon's a strange man," Dusty replied. "When you call him Comanche, it isn't far out. He's got the patience of any Injun. In all the years we rode together, he never talked much about Kliddoe; but, every time we took a trail herd north, I reckon he hoped to meet up with him. If we hadn't one day, he'd have asked Ole Devil if he could go out and return the letter. And that would have been the end of it."

They rode on in silence for a time, but Thora was too full of happiness to try and hold anything back. "You knew all along that I was hiding something, didn't you?"

"Sure, even half-guessed what it was. That was your third reason for wanting to come on this drive."

"Yes. I didn't know we would meet up with Kliddoe. And I thought, if we did, that I might be able to prevent bloodshed." Her face flushed red, but she had to talk and so went on. "My other reason is, I wrote a book about ranch life. It's selling well. I wanted to do another about trail drive work."

"A book about *this* drive?" Dusty looked startled.

She nodded, her eyes gleamed with delight. "Don't worry—I won't put anything in it to embarrass you and the boys. I didn't when I wrote my last book about the Rocking H."

"A book—all this bunch in a book. Folks won't believe it."

The Ysabel Kid halted his horse and waited for the other two to catch up with him. "Waal, that's Mr. Toon and Colonel Kliddoe done handled. Don't but leave us Marshal Earp to tend to."

"That's right." It was a shock to Thora to suddenly remember Earp's warning to the herd. "What do you aim to do about him, Dusty?"

"Nothing."

"Nothing?" Thora stared at the trail boss. "But he——"

"He's in Dodge, and we're not there yet, so how can we do anything about him?"

"But how about when we get there?"

"Ah!" Dusty looked wisely at the Kid. "That's some different, isn't it, Lon?"

"Sure. Earp's made a lot of talk about the Rocking H not coming to Dodge, but he can't back it none. Earp never was a fighting man, except when he's got the backing. Which same he won't have in Dodge. He won't try and touch us, now he's lost the edge."

It was Dusty who explained: "Dodge gets its money from three sets of folk! Texas trail drives, buffalo hunters and railroad men. So they want us in there—not chased off by some two-bit loudmouth."

"And it means that, if he chouses us off, the big, brave Mr. Earp won't never get no shiny badge to pin on his chest—which same he wants so bad. See, Mr. Earp dearly loves to hide behind a star," the Kid finished.

"You mean there won't be trouble?"

"Didn't say that," Dusty warned. "Earp could likely get some help, happen he tried. I don't figure Luke Short, Billy Tilghman, or Bat Masterson will side him in this, but he might get some others to join in. But apart from those three there isn't one he could get who'd worry a weaned calf. Up to and including Doc Holliday."

"Doc Holliday?" Thora frowned. "He's a dangerous killer, isn't he?"

The Ysabel Kid laughed, his wild Comanche laughter ringing out. "Ole Doc? Ain't never killed anybody that I knows of. He knows how to look mean and happen he got loaded enough with brave-maker, he'd kill a drunk, but that's all."

"Bat Masterson doesn't like Doc; he'd be real pleased to get a chance to move him on again. Could do it, too," said Dusty.

They came up toward the herd; the hands had for once forgotten all about cattle as they gathered round the raiding party to hear the news. Mark rode out to meet his friends. He grinned as he saw the looks Dusty was giving the crew.

"Meet Kliddoe?" he asked.

"Sure. See you've still got some of the herd."

"Nope, we lost all our'n. These belong to CA."

"Way this lot are sat round, I'd say that was to be expected," Dusty growled and rode by. Thora called that she was headed for the wagon and rode back along the line.

"What happened?" Mark inquired of the Kid.

"You should have seen it, Ole Kliddoe allowed to get himself a real edge. Offered to take on all hands with a saber."

"Poor man." Mark suffered no illusions about Dusty's skill with a saber. "I surely hope he knows better now."

"He l'arned. He l'arned."

The trail crew were all excitedly talking and none noticed the grim-faced trail boss as they listened to Billy Jack's stirring story of what happened to Kliddoe.

"Gentlemen!" The voice was cold and grimly incisive. The hands all turned to meet a pair of unpleasant grey eyes. "May I ask just what the hell you were hired for? I might be wrong when I allow it's to ride herd, not to sit on your tired butt ends and whittlewhang like old women at a dance." The crew looked sheepishly at each other and Dusty's voice rose to an angry roar: "Let's get the herd to Dodge, then you can talk your fool tongues out."

The remuda was scattered, for Lil Jackie was with the other hands. The youngster sat his horse and listened, tight lipped but unspeaking as Dusty told him in pungent and hide-searing terms just what he thought of a wrangler who allowed the remuda to scatter damned near back to Texas.

Dusty caught one of his string and saddled it, then looked round to make sure everything was meeting with his approval. The hands were shifting the cattle once more, and the remuda was collected. Then he headed back to the wagons. Thora's excited story of the raid was interrupted in midflight by a voice. "Howdy, Mr. Ballew," Dusty greeted sarcastically, almost mildly. "Would it be asking too much for you and your fool louse to get moving so that comes bedding time you've got a meal for the hands?"

Salt twisted round to observe the trail boss eyeing him. "Yes, sir, Cap'n. I means no, sir, Cap'n. I'll do just that."

"Today'd be real nice," Dusty growled. "I know Thora here's a woman and can't help jawing, but you're a man and can."

Thora poked her tongue out, turned her horse and headed for the herd. Halfway there, she remembered that she had not changed mounts and turned for the remuda. She found Lil Jackie subdued, but not over worried by the bawling out.

Dusty sat easily in his kak and watched Hobie sprinting to his wagon. Then, hearing a horse approach he turned to find the Ysabel Kid riding up. He looked the dark youngster over in disgust and said, "Huh! The scout, and what may Mr. Loncey Dalton Ysabel be scouting back here?"

"Now don't you go abusing me, Cap'n, suh," the Kid warned. "You'll likely make me wet my pants. I heerd all the ruckus down here and thought the Injuns had jumped us. It warn't but you abusing the poor, fool ole cook. I'll light out after we've had a bite to eat."

"Thank you most to death," Dusty replied. He turned in his saddle to look round and make sure everyone was working. Seeing nothing to offend his sense of things, he relaxed. "There's no need for you to go out. Besides, Thora told me she aims to write a book about the drive, and wants to know all about trail driving."

"Not from me she don't!" The Kid was emphatic. "I don't want my name in no book."

"Why not? I'll ask her to write you up real good. She can tell a few lies about you. Make you out a real nice young feller instead of a dead mean ole Comanche Dog soldier."

"It ain't the lies that'd worry me," the Kid objected. "She might tell the truth about me."

"Well, who'd that hurt?"

"*Me!* If word gets out I've been herding legal cattle, and by daylight, all my kin down on the border'll cut me dead when they see me."

Dusty slapped the Kid on the shoulder. "Say, now we've got these loafers to work, happen we'd best head up to the point and tell Mark what happened today."

Salt watched Dusty and the Kid ride off toward the point and pulled aside to allow his assistant to catch alongside. Hobie gave a scared glance ahead to make sure the trail boss couldn't see them idling, then waited to hear what his lord and master had to say.

For a time Salt Ballew was silent. Then he spat out his chaw of tobacco and spoke: "If you lives to be as old as me, which same ain't likely, you'll never work for a better man than him. He ain't tall, and he ain't the loudest talking man you'll ever see. But son, he's a trail boss."

The chuck wagon lurched forward again and Hobie started his own team to follow. The cook's louse wasn't given to deep thinking, but he agreed with what Salt had just said.

Captain Fog was a trail boss.

CHAPTER THIRTEEN

Mr. Odham Has a Plan

Dodge City got the news over the prairie grapevine. A trail drive was within two days of the town. The word ran through the saloons, gambling houses, dance halls and other places of business around the cowboy capital. They heard the word from the former Kliddoe tax collectors. That Kliddoe was dead interested them but little: he had been a menace who had slowed down the flow of money into the town. Of the words in the letter they took little interest; the War was long over and Texas money was badly needed in town.

Throughout Dodge the news was greeted with hurried checks on the items for sale.

It was a time of feverish activity in Dodge, the local citizens making the preparations. Doc Holliday spent time practicing with his new, shiny faro box, checking that it would, in the words of the crooked gambling house catalog: *"Bear any inspection while ensuring the top card was always under control and would prevent any flash from the bottom card whilst it was being dealt."*

At the Texas House, first call of every herd crew, Sam Snenton cleaned the head of his famous SS brand, in readiness for burning his mark on the sourdough keg of each spread. His pretty, dark wife, Selina, ran a final check that the kitchen held all the choice delicacies the Texans and the cattle buyers would require and ran an approving eye over the eight pretty girls who waited at the tables.

The cattle buyers were there, well-dressed men from the Eastern syndicates. They came in for the season, wallets bulging with notes and bank drafts, ready to buy the long-horned cattle the Texans brought into the shipping pens.

Maurice Odham wasn't one of the big buyers. He was a hanger-on, like a wolf following the flanks of a buffalo herd. He would hang on in Dodge, ready to flash in and cut any small profit he could for himself. He reached Dodge a week or so before the big buyers, in the hope that a small herd might turn up for him to buy. In the time he spent wandering round the saloon, he heard much that interested him. Now, as he made his way to the Texas House on Trail Street, he had an inspiration.

The Texas House was faced, across the street, by Ed Sciffen's Buffalo House. The Texas House was Odham's original destination, but he remembered all he had heard. The man he wanted to see was not to be found in Sam Snenton's place.

Crossing the street, the small cattle buyer pushed open the batwing doors of the Buffalo House and looked round. The man he wanted was standing at the bar. Wyatt Earp glanced at Odham, then ignored him. The big cattle buyers were important people in Dodge, and Earp was always polite to them. Odham wasn't one of the important ones and could have no use to anyone with plans, so Earp ignored him.

"Howdy, Marshal Earp." Odham knew the other liked to be addressed as if he was a regular marshal. "Barkeep, two drinks."

"What do you want, Odham?" Earp growled.

"I heard the Rocking H was down trail. They didn't take your warning. They'll be here in a day or so."

Earp grunted and moodily took his drink. He knew Rocking H were coming, knew it all too well. "So?"

"Well, after all you've said about them, folks are wondering what you aim to do."

"When I'm ready, I'll tell them," Earp replied. Yet, for all of that, he knew what he was going to do. When definite word had reached Dodge that Rocking H were headed for the shipping-pens, and would be first herd in, Earp had made a round of the town. He had found a startling lack of enthusiasm among his friends when he mentioned stopping the herd.

He'd tried every man he could think of, knowing that tophands would be needed to handle the crew of the Rocking H. Luke Short, Doc Holliday, Dave Mathers, they all had the same answer: They didn't aim to stop the first herd coming in, as they were feeling the financial pinch along with the rest of the citizens of Dodge. The final blow had been delivered by Bat Masterson, sheriff of Ford County. Bat and Earp were friends, but the sheriff had his position to think about. He was a different kind of man from Earp, with none of the other's sanctimonious piety. More, he was popular with all classes in Dodge, liked and respected by the Texans as a fair and honest man. Bat's words struck a chill into Earp's heart. The City Fathers didn't consider it advisable to hire Earp as assistant deputy marshal any more. They would also look with some disfavor at a man who caused any delay in the arrival of the first herd.

So Earp found himself in an unenviable position. He had sent word out against the Rocking H, in the assumption that Ben Holland would not last the long trip back to Texas—or, if he did, couldn't send a herd again for some time. Now Earp was left, without the protection of a law badge, to face the consequences.

Odham watched Earp's face, then turned to the bartender. "Any skin hunters left around town?"

"Shag Moxel and his boys," the bar-dog answered. "They lost their stake, bucking the tiger. Camped over toward the creek."

"Thanks!" Odham murmured and left the room.

For a time Earp stood silent. Then he tossed some money on the bar. "Len, I've got to go down track to Kansas City for a few days. If Shag and his boys come in, let them drink that up."

Len watched Earp leave the room and dropped the glasses into the tub under the counter.

Odham drove the livery barn buggy across the range at a fast clip. He whistled a tune and watched the cloud of dust which marked the progress of the first herd to Dodge. In his mind was an idea that he had used many times before in other trail-end towns. They had been good days—just at the start of the trail herds when every man who could throw a herd together in Texas did so and headed north.

The livery barn horse kept up a steady trot. Odham handled the reins with half his attention on what he would say to the woman who owned the herd. The crew might not listen to him, but she would.

A tall, black-dressed young man, riding a big white stallion, was approaching. Odham watched him and decided he would be the scout for the herd.

The Ysabel Kid studied the buggy with some interest, his red-hazel eyes taking in every detail. He rode forward and halted his horse across the path of the buggy.

"Howdy!" he greeted.

"Where at's your herd?"

"Under the dust there, less'n they lost 'em all," the Kid replied. "You're a cattle buyer ain't you?"

"I am." Odham puffed out his chest pompously. This cowhand was regarding him with less favor than a cattle buyer deserved. "How's the drive been?"

"Fair. I saw you one time in Hays."

This wasn't what Odham had expected; he had hoped that none of the hands would know him. Certainly, he now hoped none would know of his business methods while in Hays City.

"I want to see your boss," he remarked, as casually as he could.

"Take you back to see him."

Dusty, Mark and Thora were riding out ahead of the herd. They were relaxed and taking things easy over the last few miles. Mark left the point to Kiowa and Billy Jack, claiming that, as he missed out on all the fun, he was going to take things easy for the last few miles of the drive.

"Won't make Dodge today," Dusty remarked. "We'll bed down out there a piece, and take the herd in tomorrow. Be there around noon."

"Why'd you have a double night herd and both scouts out last night?" Thora asked. "I thought we were out of trouble."

"Just being careful. There used to be a bunch working the trail-end towns. They laid up a few miles out and hit the herds, stampeded them on either the last night or the second last. They'd usually get away with a few dozen head, or more. See, the trail crews weren't expecting trouble that near to the town."

"What'd they do with the cattle?"

"Hold them to the end of the season, then run them in. They'd try to alter, or counterbrand, the cattle. There were some buyers who would take a herd without asking too many questions."

"Yeah!" Mark put in. He was looking ahead at the Kid and the man who drove the buggy alongside him. "And one of them's coming up right now."

Dusty looked at the man in the buggy, his memory for faces being as good as those of his two friends. He recognized the newcomer. A half-smile played around his lips as he guessed why Odham was coming. "Sure, Mark, we know him. I wonder if he's going to try his old game on us?"

"He'd never chance it," Mark scoffed.

"What game is that?" Thora asked.

Before the Texans could reply, the buggy was up to them. Odham might have wondered why such a small, insignificant man rode at the place of honor, but he knew this man. "Howdy, Cap'n Fog. I'm Maurice Odham. We met in Hays, I think."

"I remember." There was little friendship in Dusty's voice.

"I'd like to talk with the owner."

"This is Mrs. Holland."

Odham raised his hat politely, a warm, ingratiating smile on his face. He glanced at the cattle going past, fat, well-meated stock. They would command a high price in Dodge City. If he could play his cards right, the price would roll into his pockets.

"Mrs. Holland, I came out here to talk business with you. After seeing your herd, I'm really sorry to tell you that it isn't safe for you to take them into Dodge City."

"Not take them into Dodge?" Thora glanced at Dusty and Mark—they looked impassive, but Dusty winked at her. "Why shouldn't we take my herd into Dodge? I'm sorry we can't offer you a meal, unless you can stay until we bed down."

"That won't be necessary. What I came here for was to save you the embarrassment that awaits you. I will buy your herd from you right now."

"Buy the herd?" Thora felt foolish repeating the words but couldn't think of anything else to say. Dusty and Mark weren't helping her with their silence. "But that isn't usual, is it?"

"Not under normal circumstances. I would have waited in Dodge. But when I heard that Marshal Earp was taking on men to stop your herd using the pens, I thought I would come out and meet you, buy the herd and save you any further trouble. After all it is common knowledge that Marshal Earp ordered you never to use this town again. When a man of his caliber gives you such an order it is hardly prudent to go against it."

"I didn't think Earp could prevent our using Dodge," Thora objected but she was beginning to see the light now. Dusty and Mark still kept their faces impassive and unreadable and the Kid lounged in his saddle looking more Indian than ever.

"He can't under law of course, but in Dodge he and Sheriff Masterson are the law. You know of how they stick together. I saw Marshal Earp leaving the sheriff's office only yesterday, I daresay he'd been making arrangements to stop your herd coming to Dodge. I realize that your men could fight their way in—but think of the trouble and the bloodshed."

"How much a head you figger on paying?" Dusty put in.

"Well, I have to hire the men to——"

"How much?"

"Fifteen dollars. I will have to——"

"*All* of fifteen dollars?" Dusty looked amazed at such generosity. "Why thank you 'most to death."

"That's real neighborly of you, friend," Mark agreed; but his voice held irony, not gratitude. "You rode all these miles out here to take the herd off our hands, and save Thora some trouble. I allow we owe you a vote of thanks. What do you reckon, Lon?"

The Ysabel Kid looked Odham over with the same kind of pleasure he might give a bed-sharing Gila monster. Pushing the big white to the buggy, he leaned forward to look Odham over. "Yep, let's us give him one right now. Just like ole Stone Hart's Wedge did that time at Hays. Mister, you've got a heart like a winter's night— cold, dark and hawg dirty!"

"What's wrong, Dusty?" Thora asked, though she had a fair idea.

"Not much. This kind-hearted gent here come all the way from Dodge, with us less than a day's drive out, and offers to buy the herd from us."

"Sure," Mark finished. "For less than half we can make for it in Dodge."

"Mrs. Holland, I'd prefer to deal with you, not hired hands. I came out here to save you from some trouble——"

"You came to make some easy money," the Kid growled. "Now just take off, or I'll ram a boot down your neck."

Odham scowled and only his knowledge of the ways of Loncey Dalton Ysabel prevented further objections. He scowled round at the herd, then back at Thora. "I'm sorry you take this attitude, Mrs. Holland. I've tried to help you, but——"

"I'm sorry, too. But, when I took Dusty on as trail boss, I agreed that he would handle the herd. I'm merely Rocking H's rep, and so I've no more to say about selling the herd than any other hand. If you want to buy the cattle, you must talk with Captain Fog."

Odham scowled, for he knew that what Thora said was the truth. If she was riding as the representative of the spread, she could not sell the herd; only the trail boss could do that. He also knew that any attempt to fool, or buy cattle from Dusty Fog was doomed for disaster straight off. Turning the buggy, he set the horse moving and drove back across the range toward Dodge.

Away from the herd, he laid his whip to the horse and let it run. In his heart, there was black rage against the Texas men who rode for Rocking H. His plan had been to persuade Thora to sell and they foiled it neatly.

The horses were lathered by the time he reached Dodge; circling the town, he found what he was looking for.

The camp of the buffalo hunters was on the bank of a creek—just a wagon, a fire and some untidy bedrolls. The seven men who lounged around the fire were all dressed in buckskins, dirty and unshaven. One was tall, heavily built and ugly looking. He looked up as Odham drove up to the fire. "What do you want?" he growled.

"You Shag Moxel?" Odham knew the answer without needing the surly nod the other gave him. "How's things, Shag?"

"Not bad." Moxel took the whisky flask Odham offered, drank and then spat appreciatively. "You from Dodge?"

"Sure. I saw the trail boss of the Rocking H. He's looking for you."

The skin hunters looked up from their places round the fire. Shag Moxel's brows drew into lines as he asked, "Is he now?"

"Reckon we can handle him, don't you, Shag?" one of the other men asked.

"Could, if we'd gotten enough food to stay on," Moxel agreed. "There ain't no hunting round Dodge, and we've got to head out after the herds."

Odham took out his wallet, peeled off some notes and passed them to Moxel. "Here. Call it a loan. Go into town and get yourself some food. You watch for their trail boss. You can't miss him—he rides a paint."

Moxel took the money and looked up suspiciously. "Why're you doing this for us?"

"I don't like cowhands. Besides, we don't want folks saying you ran out of Dodge and from the Texans."

Moxel reached over and picked up the old ten-gauge shotgun from his bedroll. He broke open the weapon. "Nope—we don't."

Thora watched the cattle buyer heading away, then turned her attention to the three lounging Texas men. "Just what was all that about?" she asked. "I didn't get half of it."

"I never thought he'd pull that old game with us," Mark replied. "It went out with the Colt Dragoon."

"What game?"

"One he played a couple of times, maybe more, in the early drive days. He'd leave Hays, or whatever town Kliddoe was working near, and look for a small herd, one without many men. Then he'd warn them Kliddoe was waiting and offer to buy the herd," Mark explained.

"At about half the market price," Dusty put in.

"Sure. Worked real well, for a piece. The small owners hadn't the men to fight off Kliddoe, and couldn't afford to pay, so they sold to Odham and reckoned they were lucky. Odham worked it well. Then he made a mistake. The small ranchers back to Texas pooled together. Stone Hart gathered their herds, made a big drive and came north. He faced Kliddoe down, him and his Wedge crew. Then, the following day, Odham met him with the news Kliddoe was ahead and reckoned he'd buy the herd. Wedge sent him back to Hays without his pants!"

"He just faded out after that, turned up in a couple of other trail towns, but word had gone out about him. The small owners didn't try to drive alone; they pooled and hired Stone Hart's Wedge, or somebody like that, to bring their cattle to market," Dusty finished.

Dude and Lil Jackie rode up. The cowhand raised his

hat to Thora and asked, "Can the button head into Dodge, Cap'n? There's some of us left without smoke or chaw."

Dusty studied the eager face of the youngster, then glanced down at the fancy Navy Colt stuck in his belt. Lil Jackie had changed almost beyond recognition since joining the herd. Salt's cooking, and plenty of it, gave him a filled-out look. The trail hands, with typical cowboy generosity, had supplied him with a change of clothing. Dude had given the wrangler a good hat and burned the old woolsey which caused him to be drenched with stew and knocked down by the trail boss.

The boy had changed; he looked older, fitter, and was well able to handle himself in either the rough horseplay of the camp or the hard work of the remuda. He sat his paint horse and waited eagerly to hear his fate.

"All right, boy," Dusty said. "Bring me a sack of Bull Durham and don't you get yourself into any trouble. If I find you in jail when we get to Dodge, I'll take the hide off you."

Lil Jackie whooped his delight, kicked his spurs into the ribs of his horse and headed off for Dodge. Dusty watched him go and then turned to the Kid. "Ain't no more scouting to be done, is there?"

"Nope. You reckon I'd best go to Dodge after the button and see he stays out of trouble?"

"Reckon you'd best watch the remuda. See they keep out of trouble."

CHAPTER FOURTEEN

Shag Moxel's Indiscretion

"The button not back yet?" Dusty asked as he stood eating his breakfast on the last day of the drive.

"Not yet. Likely stayed in Dodge the night and's headed back now," Mark replied, then looked round the camp. "Reckon we'll make Dodge this week, happen this bunch don't fall asleep on the trail."

The cowhands jeered derisively and headed for their horses. There was a lighthearted mood in the air as they headed the cattle up ready to pull out on the last stage of the journey. Every man was thinking of the various uses they had for the money they'd get when the herd paid off.

Kiowa and Tarbrush handled the remuda this final day, leaving the Kid to ride ahead with Dusty and Mark. It was the last day and already, in the far distance, they could see the sun shining on the roofs of Dodge City.

The Kid stopped his horse, squinting his eyes as he stared ahead across the range.

"Two riders," he said, pointing across the range. "Sits like Bat Masterson and Billy Tilghman."

Dusty and Mark could see the two riders, but not well enough to make any guess as to who they might be. They both felt admiration for their keen-eyed friend and knew his guess was most likely correct.

"Best go and meet them, then," Dusty suggested. "They'll likely want to warn us not to rope Trail Street and haul it down to the Cimmaron."

Masterson and Tilghman rode toward the Texans, and neither man looked over-eager for this meeting. They knew that there were stormy times ahead, and hoped they could stop the worst of it.

"Howdy, Bat, Billy!" Dusty greeted. There were few Yankee lawmen he would have greeted so warmly. These two were good, honest lawmen; both played fairly with the Texas men, and so gained Dusty's respect for he knew handling trail hands at the end of a drive was exacting and dangerous work.

"Howdy, Dusty!" Masterson replied. He felt definitely uneasy and glanced at Billy Tilghman. "We've got some bad news for you."

"Mr. Earp ain't gone and died of his meanness, has he?" the Kid inquired, watching the two lawmen with the wary attention of a part-reformed border smuggler.

Masterson didn't smile; his face was grave, his eyes not meeting those of the Texan. "You sent your wrangler into Dodge last night?"

"Sure," Dusty felt uneasy. Masterson was a good enough friend not to be nervous like this. "Don't tell me you had to throw him into the hoosegow for treeing the town."

"No. He's been killed!"

"Little Jackie—dead!" The easy slouch had left Dusty now.

"When did it happen, and how?" The slit-eyed, mean Comanche look was on the Kid's face again and the savage growl in his voice.

"Last night, he was riding out of town and got shot in the back."

"With a ten-gauge?" Dusty's voice dropped to a soft drawl, but Masterson had heard it go soft like that before. When it did, the time had come for trouble. It meant bad trouble, and hunt for the cyclone cellars.

"With a ten-gauge," Tilghman agreed. He was one of the bravest men ever to wear a law badge but he knew he wouldn't face any of this trio in their present mood.

"Where at's Earp?" the Kid's savage, Comanche growl cut in.

"He left town on the noon train yesterday. I saw him go," Masterson replied.

"How about Shag Moxel?" Dusty put in, accepting Masterson's word.

"Still in Dodge. Saw him at the Buffalo House. His bunch allow he was with them all night. Sciffen reckons they were playing poker in his back room. We can't prove anything——"

"Prove?" The Kid spat the word out. "Had it been Earp or one of his stinking *amigos* who got downed, there wouldn't be no looking for proof. It'd just be find the first Texas neck and stretch it."

"Not while I'm wearing a badge," Masterson snapped, his temper rising. "I tried to find out who killed your boy. Give me time and I may yet do it."

"No offense, Bat," the Kid replied. "I just feel mean as a razorback hawg. We took that kid on in Texas and brought him north. He worked hard and was making a hand. Then some lousy back-shooting skunk puts him under."

Thora rode across to the party; she could read the signs real well for a Yankee gal, and she knew that, when Dusty stopped lounging in his saddle, trouble was coming.

"Jackie dead?" she gasped when Dusty told her. "Who did it?"

"I don't know, but it's surely time we found out."

"Hold hard now, Dusty. Moxel's got six men with him. I don't want no war starting in Dodge." Masterson snapped.

Dusty faced the sheriff, his eyes cold and expressionless. "You should have told that to the man who killed Jackie. *Before* he did it."

"Wasn't the button riding his paint?" Mark's deep drawl cut in.

"Sure." Tilghman knew trouble was coming and wanted to stop it if he could. "We've got it in the city——"

The words died an uneasy death as Tilghman and every man here looked at the huge paint stallion Dusty sat.

"Hell!" Masterson spat out. "That buckshot was meant for you."

"And there'll likely be more of it," Dusty replied. Turning to Thora he went on. "I want——"

"Take every man, if you need them," she answered, before he could finish. "I want the men who killed Jackie."

"Won't need but Mark and Lon. You aiming to stop us, Bat?"

Masterson sat silent for a time. He knew that any attempt to halt Dusty, Mark and the Kid would end in gunplay. Then he shook his head; it wasn't fear that made him take this attitude, but his sense of fairness. The murder last night had been aimed at Dusty, not at the wrangler. Dusty would be in danger, unless he found the murderer, and found him real fast.

"No, Dusty, I'm not going to stop you. I let Moxel stay on when I should have run him out of town. I was near certain he gunned Ben down and hoped I'd get some proof. He kept quiet, and then this happened."

"It was Moxel then?"

"I don't know enough to take him to court, but he's a friend of Sciffen. And his bunch would say whatever he told them. The town's yours for three weeks. Billy and me aims to go round the county on tax assessment. You'll be gone when we get back, I reckon."

"We'll be gone," Dusty agreed. "Us and Clay Allison both."

Masterson nodded. "Heard he's coming north. I also heard some damned fool says I've passed word that he shouldn't use Dodge. I never passed any word."

Dusty knew this without being told. He could guess that the story had been spread by someone who wanted to see a gunfight or wanted some excitement. "I'll tell ole Clay."

Masterson knew that, if he stayed in Dodge, there would be shooting and while not being afraid of Allison, was a realist. If he killed Allison, a lot of other men were going to look for him, and the reputation he gained.

If he died, the City Fathers of Dodge would give him a first-rate funeral, but would only mourn him long enough to put in a replacement sheriff.

This way he could be out of Dodge while Clay Allison was there and not lose face by it.

The Kid jerked his rifle free and kicked his white forward, then stopped in disgust. The others all turned to see a fast-departing man headed for Dodge.

"Who was it?" Thora asked.

"A skin hunter. He must have followed you, to see what was happening, Bat," the Kid replied. "That proves Moxel shot Jackie."

"Likely," Dusty agreed. "Thora, you're trail boss. Billy Jack'll be segundo. Keep the herd moving. We'll meet you outside Dodge." Turning to the other two members of Ole Devil's floating outfit he snapped, "Let's go!"

Thora watched the three young men riding toward Dodge, then turned back to the lawmen. "I think we could offer you breakfast and coffee back at the wagon, if we hurry."

"Thanks, Mrs. Holland. Like to say that Dodge City wasn't behind the word Wyatt put out about Rocking H. There's times I think Wyatt talks too much."

The skin hunter who had followed Masterson and Tilghman from Dodge made good time back to Dodge. He pulled up outside the Buffalo House, leaped up the steps and crashed through the doors.

"You were right, Shag. Masterson went to the Texans and told them."

Moxel turned. "That means they'll be coming after us."

Apart from Moxel's men, only the owner, Ed Sciffen, and his barman, Len, were in the saloon. Word had gone round Dodge that trouble was coming and, with that strange premonition which was peculiar to the frontier crowds, people stayed clear of both the Buffalo House and Sam Snenton's Texas House across the street.

Sciffen, a contrast to the untidy, dirty skin hunters with his elegant gambler dress, looked worried.

"What you aiming to do, Shag?" he asked. "You got the wrong man last night."

"I was telled the gunslick rode a paint. When I saw a Texas man riding a paint, and toting a fancy gun, I reckoned he was the one."

"It wasn't Dusty Fog," Sciffen warned. "But he'll be here, looking for you."

"We stopping to fight?" a tall, gangling skin hunter asked.

"Sure, but we takes them *our* way," Moxel replied, leering round at the others. "Where'll be the first place them Texans head for, if they come looking for us?"

"Texas House, like they allus does," Len suggested.

"That's right. We've seen all them Dodge City John Laws pull out after Masterson went. Them Texans won't go to the jail, having seed Masterson. They'll come straight to the Texas House and ask Snenton where we are. I wants Blinky and Herb up on the roof. Bert and Case'll be along the street a piece, one on each side. Then we'll have 'em."

"Snenton'll warn them," a man growled.

"No, he won't. 'Cause you'n Moe'll be in thar with a gun lined on that pretty wife that Snenton's so fond of. All right, Rut?"

Rut nodded, then went on: "Where'll you be?"

"Right here at the bar. Me'n ole Len's going to have our ten-gauges lined on that door. That'll be the only way the Texans can run. Where you going, Sciffen?"

The saloon-keeper had left the bar and was walking across the room. He stopped. "Got me some office work to do in the back."

"All right. But, happen you don't come out when the shooting starts, I'll burn your place down."

Sciffen tried to smile, but he was cursing the luck which made Wyatt Earp his customer. Earp had left money for Moxel's bunch to stay on with, and now Sciffen was deeper in trouble than he ever had been before. He went into the back room, opened his desk drawer and lifted out his short-barreled Webley Bulldog revolver. He knew that he had to help Moxel, whether he liked it or not.

The Texas House was empty at this early hour, and Sam Snenton was helping his wife to make the final arrangements for the arrival of the cattle buyers at lunch time. Snenton was tall, wide shouldered and heavily built. He was a happy man, dressed in a spotless white shirt and comfortable jeans. Around his waist was an apron; but, tucked in his waistband out of sight, was a Remington double derringer.

The place was quiet except for the occasional noise made by Hop Lee, the Chinese cook and general handyman, working in the kitchen. The dining room was large, and tables were large enough to accommodate six men each. Behind the bar, burned in the woodwork, were many brands—for this was the first place every Texas trail drive crew made for when they hit Dodge at the end of the drive. Nearly every ranch owner in Texas had left his brand burned on the wall backboard. Among them was P. and C. brand of Mark Counter's father's Big Bend outfit. In a place of honor was the OD Connected brand of Ole Devil Hardin. Snenton was proud of that backboard; it had come with him from Hays, Abilene and Wichita. On hooks made from the horns of a Texas steer hung the famous brand he used to mark the sourdough kegs of the different spreads which came to Dodge.

Selina Snenton was small, dark haired and pretty. It was her capable business sense that turned this place into a financial success, for Sam was a genial host and liable to forget to collect pay for the meals eaten by a crew. She brought a solvency to the business, while he handled any trouble with a fast-pulled gun, or a punch like a Missouri mule kick.

Two men entered the dining room. She turned and frowned. They were skin hunters, part of Moxel's bunch. "We're not serving yet, gentlemen," she said.

Snenton turned and frowned; he disliked the Moxel bunch and tried to keep them out of his place. "Best come back in a couple of hours, if you want food. We won't have any until then."

The men moved to either side of the door, both drawing their guns. Rut growled: "Just stand still, Sammywell, and nobody'll get hurt."

Snenton did what any man with gun-savvy would have under the circumstances. He stood still, but his hand dropped casually toward his waistband. "What's the——?" he asked softly.

"Stand real still, Sammywell, if you don't want the missus hurt," Moe snarled, cocking his gun and lining it on Selina. At that range he could hardly have missed.

"All right. But, if this is a stickup, you've picked a real poor time. We banked last night."

"Ain't sticking you up, Sam," Moe answered. "We wants to wait here for some friends what's likely to arrive sudden and unwelcomed if we don't do it for 'em."

"Friends?" Sam Snenton felt suddenly cold. He had heard of the killing of the Texas boy and guessed why the skin hunters were here. "Your friends wouldn't come here."

"These friends would. See, they're them Texans what's coming after ole Shag for killing their pard last night." Moe had been drinking and was slack jawed because of it.

"Moe!" Rut growled. "Shut your face and get across the room. Set at that table with your gun on Miz Snenton. Set down, ma'am. I'll keep watch out the winder."

Selina sat at the table and the man took a chair near her, his gun resting on the top of the table. She looked down at the cloth and asked, "Did Moxel kill that boy last night?"

"Sure. Allowed it was Dusty Fog, after him for gunning Ben Holland last year," Moe replied. "Ole Shag'd downed Holland, but the charge was weak."

"Why did Moxel shoot Ben Holland?" Snenton asked casually.

"Shag don't like Texas men. He heard Holland was tough and wanted to try him out." Moe grinned as he talked, a drunken leer. "Last night he saw that kid on the paint. He figgered it was like the little fat feller said. Dusty Fog was in town looking for him, so he got out his ole ten-gauge and dropped the boy."

"And you reckon to take Dusty out here?" Snenton watched the men, awaiting his chance. "Knowing Dusty, he'll head straight to the jail, to ask Bat Masterson instead of coming here."

"Naw, they won't," Rut sneered. "Ole Shag's real smart. He had Bert follow Masterson and Tilghman out of town. They went to the herd to tell them Texans. They'll come here first. Ole Shag's smart—he'll take him some reb scalps."

"Like hell!" Snenton scoffed. "Moxel's no good without it's dark and he's behind a man."

"Yeah?" Rut was bursting with misplaced pride in his boss. "He knows they'll come here fust. He's got the sweetest lil ole gun trap a man ever saw laid on here. Two boys up the street, two on the roof of the Buffler House. Me'n Moe here, and him in the saloon—at the bar with the bar-dog and two scatters. We've got them rebs whipsawed."

Snenton knew to be sure; from the window he could see the two men moving on the Buffalo House roof. He also knew, as did Moxel, that the Texas men would come here looking for information. That was as natural for a Texas man in Dodge as it would be for a homing pigeon to make its way back to the loft it left. The three or more Texas men would come riding toward the Texas House—right into an ambush that gave them no chance of escape.

Snenton tried to sound mocking, but he knew the skin hunters were right in their thinking. "You don't reckon Dusty Fog'll fall for a play like that?" he asked. "The skin hunter doesn't live who can do anything better than Dusty Fog. He'll bust your trap, like it wasn't there."

"Be that so?" Moe growled. "Well, when they buries

them Texans you'll know you wuss wrong."

"They're coming, Moe." Rut's voice was urgent. "Folks's clearing Trail Street."

Selina watched the man at the table. He was sweating now. She waited for a chance to do something, for she knew, and liked, Dusty Fog.

Rut pulled a handkerchief out and rubbed the sweat from his face. He shoved the bandanna back into his pocket and rubbed his palm against his trouser leg.

"Scared, Rut?" Snenton asked. "Don't reckon it'll work now, do you?"

Rut snarled a curse and looked back out of the window. He knew the reputation of those three Texas men who would be leading the attacking party. If there was the slightest flaw in their plans, things would be going real bad for Shag Moxel's men.

From the kitchen came a wailing, high sound, which bit into Rut's nerves like a red-hot knife. He had never heard Hop Lee, Snenton's help, singing, or he would have known that this was an Oriental version of some popular ballad.

"What the hell is that?" Moe croaked.

"Our kitchen help," Selina answered, her hand dropping below the level of the table and holding the edge of the cloth.

Rut roared out for the man to be quiet, but Hop Lee was used to the Occidental barbarians showing a lack of appreciation for music. He had long since learned the only thing to do was ignore them and carry right on with his song.

"Lee doesn't know any English," Selina remarked.

The skin hunters listened to the wailing notes for a time. It was bad enough waiting for the Texans, without having that banshee call jarring at the nerves. Rut gave in. "You know how to make him understand?" Selina nodded. "Then stop him—and quick."

That was what Selina had wanted Rut to say; she and her husband both knew Hop Lee spoke good enough English. Speaking in the fluent Mandarin dialect Hop

Lee had taught her, Selina gave rapid orders. The singing stopped abruptly. The room was silent, except for the ticking of the wall clock. The two skin hunters were sweating freely now, both wondering why Shag Moxel had chosen to remain in the comparative safety of the Buffalo House, instead of fighting out on the street. The bottle-poured Bravemaker was laying cold on them.

"They're coming down Trail Street now!" Rut hissed. "Keep that gun lined on the woman."

Snenton half turned; he saw the kitchen door slowly opening, a slim yellow hand pushing it. Catching his wife's eye, Snenton nodded. The time was coming to take action. Selina gripped the tablecloth. She was pale, her face showing the strain. Looking out of the window, she saw three men riding into view.

Moe's hand jerked as Selina heaved on the tablecloth. The gun was out of line and the woman dropped to the floor. Moe roared out and tried to bring the gun into line. At the same moment, Snenton drew and fired at Rut, missing him. Hop Lee threw open the kitchen door, his hand swinging forward, a meat cleaver flying from it. Moe's gun swung down, then he pitched to one side, the cleaver having split his head open. He was dead before he hit the ground.

Rut twisted round as the bullet slammed into the wall. He saw the double-barreled derringer in Snenton's hand. Panic hit him. He twisted back toward the door, tore it open. At the same moment Snenton roared out, "*Ambush*, Dusty!"

CHAPTER FIFTEEN

Mark Counter Throws a Barrel

The word ran round Dodge City faster than a wind-swept prairie fire. Trouble was coming soon. The Dodge City police force, those tough, rough handlers of drunks, got the word. They had seen Masterson and Tilghman go from town and took their departure right after. Not one of the police force wanted to be here when Rocking H came to town, looking for the men who had downed their pard. It wouldn't be a safe location for a lawman who was supposed to stop shootings in Dodge City.

By the time the three members of Ole Devil's floating outfit rode into town, Trail Street was as clear of human life as Death Valley on a real hot summer's afternoon. The street was deserted, not even a horse standing at the rail of a saloon. Yet, in every building, from every window, faces looked out, watching the three men riding slowly toward the Texas House.

As always in these matters, Dusty rode in the center of the trio, Mark at his right and the Kid at his left. They rode slowly, relaxed in their saddles. For all normal signs, they might have been three drifting cowhands, coming into town for a spree. The Kid alone gave the lie to that; he rested his old rifle across his knees. In affairs of this nature, he preferred his rifle to an opener and, after that, he might use his old Dragoon to take the pot. Dusty and Mark left their rifles booted; they were trained Cavalry men and preferred their Colts for combat in the saddle.

Moxel's guess had been correct in one thing and so had Snenton's. The three Texans were headed for the Texas House, but they weren't riding blindly into a trap.

All three of them sat their horses in the relaxed, easy way of the cowhand. They appeared to be looking ahead, but never had they been more alert than they were then. All could read the signs; they *knew* Moxel was waiting for them, ready and prepared to fight.

A movement and a splash of color—where no such movement, or color, should be—caught the Ysabel Kid's attention. He saw the two men on the roof of the Buffalo House an instant before Dusty and Mark picked them up.

"Two up there on the roof of the Buffler House, behind the false front." The Kid just breathed the words out.

"See them," Mark answered, just as softly. "Two more ahead there—one on either side of the street."

Dusty was silent; he too had marked the four men. The pair up on the roof were dismissed from his calculations as a factor in the game. Those two men were as good as dead; or, if they weren't, the Ysabel Kid was losing his skill with a rifle. Yet, there should be more men. Moxel had six men in his bunch, and only four were in sight. The rest might be in the Buffalo House. If that hadn't been Sam Snenton's Texas House across the street from Sciffen's place, Dusty would have expected men there, too. But Snenton would never allow a Texas man to be attacked from his place.

"Waiting for us, just like you said," Mark went on, just as quietly as before. He had long since stopped marveling at Dusty's ability for putting himself in the place of the other man, then thinking as he thought. It was an ability which had long stood Dusty in good stead, and it stood by them today.

"Yep, only four of them. The rest must be in the Buffalo House," Dusty replied. "Is Moxel out on the street?"

"Nope, he's a big, heavy *hombre*—less'n Red Tolliver called him wrong," the Kid answered. "Red allows to have known Moxel in Wichita."

They were in front of the Texas House now. All halted

their horses, knowing it wouldn't be long before the shooting started. The Kid watched the men on the roof, but his Indian intuition warned him all was not well.

From inside the Texas House a shot sounded and a voice yelled, "Ambush, Dusty!"

The Ysabel Kid left the saddle of his white in a dive, his rifle crashing even as he fell. Up on the roof one of the two men reeled back from out of cover, a hole between his eyes. Even as that man went down, all hell tore loose on Trail Street.

At the shout, Dusty and Mark sent their horses leaping forward, both drawing their guns as they charged at the two men along the street. The door of the Texas House was pulled open and a man leapt out, gun in hand.

Rut landed on the street, his revolver lining on the fast-rolling Ysabel Kid. He fired one shot, the bullet joining the dust spurts following the rolling black shape. Then a shadow fell on Rut and he heard the wild, terrifying scream of a fighting stallion. Rut twisted round. A scream broke from his lips as he saw a huge white stallion rearing over him, iron-shod hooves smashing down at him. The scream stopped as the hooves thudded home. Rut went down with the white horse, fighting screams shattered the air, smashing at him with battering hooves.

The Kid rolled over, lead licking dust spurts behind him. He rolled right up to his feet, his rifle lining up and beating a rapid tattoo. On the false front boards of the Buffalo House a line of holes formed, creeping nearer to the buffalo hunter. The eighth hole sent splinters flying into the man's face. The Kid's rifle sights lined as the skin hunter stepped back in an involuntary movement. The rifle kicked back against the black shirt and a skin hunter went down dead.

The skin hunters on either side of the street leaped out, guns coming up. Mark cut down on the one nearest to him, the long-barreled Army Colts throwing lead into him. The man slumped forward, dropping his short carbine. The other spun round, his gun fell from his fingers and he clutched up at his shoulder. Dusty rode nearer, his smoking Colts lined and ready. The skin hunter turned and ran, staggering from the pain of his wound. For an instant, he was close to death. Dusty's Colt lifted and lined, the V notch in the hammer lip and the low, white brass foresight covering the man's back. At that range, Dusty could hardly have missed. Then the Texan holstered his guns and turned the paint to head back along the street.

The Ysabel Kid lowered his smoking rifle and, for the first time, noticed the fighting screams of his white stallion. He whirled round and yelled: "Back off, Nigger! Back off there, hoss!"

The white backed away, nostrils flaring and angry snorts blowing out loudly as it pawed and stamped the bloody ground. The skin hunter wasn't a pretty sight, the white stallion's flaying hooves had shattered his head almost to a pulp.

"Kid, Snenton coming out!"

Sam Snenton wanted to come out of the Texas House and took this elementary, but necessary precaution. The Kid had seen one enemy come out of the Texas House; he wouldn't wait to argue if the door opened again to let out some other unheralded figure. Even after his yell, Snenton found the Kid's rifle lined on the door when he came out.

"Howdy, Sam. Nice company you keep in thar."

Snenton stepped out, looked down at the bloody remains of Rut and twisted his face wryly. "Moxel's in the Buffalo House," he said as Dusty and Mark rode back. "Sorry about this. They had two in my place. Didn't get a chance to warn you until just afore you stopped."

"Them two in your place, weren't but the one came out," Mark pointed out. "The other one still inside?"

"Sure."

"He going any place?" the Kid inquired.

"Nope—tangled with Hop Lee's cleaver."

The Kid grinned. He vaulted on to the hitching rail

and tried to see into the Buffalo House. Climbing down, he shook his head. "Can't see a thing in there."

"Both got a scattergun, and they'll cut down any man who goes through that door," Snenton put in. "Rut and his pard talked some."

Dusty swung down from the paint. He looked at the Buffalo House and called: "Moxel, your hired men are all dead. Come out and see how you stack against a man who's facing you."

In the saloon, Moxel licked his lips. He still stood at the bar for he had been sure that his gun trap couldn't fail. Crossing the room, he looked out of the window; the three Texans were still on their feet, and Snenton was also there. Moxel knew that his men were all done. He hefted the shotgun and moved to stand with his back to the far wall. Cocking the hammers of the heavy weapon he yelled: "Come in here and git me!"

"I'll do just that," Dusty shouted back and started forward.

Mark lunged forward, enveloping his small pard in a grip which gave Dusty no chance to struggle. "Hold hard, boy!" Mark growled. "Try any of Tommy Okasi's tricks on me, and I'll toss you through the Texas House wall. This is for us all—you can't lick two scatterguns."

"Mark's right, *amigo*," the Kid agreed. "You always keep telling me not to rush in, head down and pawing dirt."

Dusty stood still; he knew better than try and break Mark's grip on him. The big Texan was fully aware of the tricks Ole Devil's Japanese servant, Tommy Okasi, taught Dusty; but holding him like that was fairly safe.

"All right, you pair of wet hens. What do we do?"

Mark let loose. He looked round and his gaze stopped on the large water barrel which stood before the Buffalo House. The barrel was supposed to be kept full of water, in case of fire. "Is that full?" he asked.

Snenton shook his head; he was a member of the Dodge City Fire Department and knew Sciffen. "I told him to get it filled a week back, but I'd bet he hasn't."

"Good, that's all we want. Let's go. Real Army tactics."

The Kid looked puzzled; he had never been an officer as had the other two, and his sole tactic in the Army had consisted of shooting faster than any Union soldier he came across. "What the hell're you getting at?"

"It's called diversion, then attack, *amigo*," Dusty explained.

They crossed the street and halted just in front of the Buffalo House sidewalk. Mark stepped forward and looked into the barrel; it was empty. He bent and lifted the heavy object, his muscles writhing and bulging as the weight came up. "Ready?" he gritted through his teeth.

"Willing and able," Dusty replied, stepping forward on to the sidewalk.

The Kid ducked under the hitching rail and stepped up on to the sidewalk. He flattened himself against the wall by the far window. Lifting his old Dragoon, he prepared to take action.

Mark tensed, lifted the barrel up over his head and threw it right through the window. The entire pane of glass shattered and, from the dark interior of the saloon, three shotgun blasts boomed out. The barrel, hit by three heavy charges of buckshot, burst, staves flying in all directions.

From the directions of the shots, Dusty knew where the men stood in the saloon. Two shots came from the rear wall—that man's gun was empty—but only one had been fired from the bar. Dusty knew the bar-dog might still have one more shot in his weapon, but that didn't halt him.

The batwings burst open. Dusty came through in a flying dive, his old bone-handled Colt guns out ready. In his flashing dive across the room, he saw the bar-dog behind the bar; and, backed against the wall, stood a big burly man in buckskins. The bar-dog saw, too late, what the thing which smashed the window was, and he swung his shotgun round. Dusty landed on the floor and threw over a table, blocking him briefly from the man at the bar.

Moxel dropped his shotgun and clawed at the Colt in his belt. Dusty rolled over on the floor; he fired his first shot while his right shoulder was still on the floor. The second roared as he rolled on to his stomach; and a third as he went over to his left side. Moxel slammed back into the wall as the first bullet hit him. He tried to lift his gun but two more shots hammered lead into him. Slowly, he slid down the wall, his guns dropping from his hand.

Len, the bar-dog, jerked his shotgun round, then the other front window smashed. The Ysabel Kid's old Dragoon boomed from the broken pane, throwing its charge at the man behind the bar. Len felt as if a red-hot anvil had struck his arm. He spun round, the shotgun falling and crashing as it struck the ground, sending the nine buckshot charge tearing harmlessly into the roof. The bar-dog stared numbly down at the smashed, mangled remains of his arm.

Mark followed the barrel through the window. He fired fast at the man who came from the back room, short Webley Bulldog gun throwing lead at Dusty.

The lead slammed into the floor near Dusty's face. He rolled over, thumb easing back the hammer of the Army Colt. He held his fire; Mark's bullet beat him. Sciffen, the owner, hit the wall, blood oozing from a hole in his shoulder. He dropped his gun and screamed at the Texans not to shoot him.

"You all right, Dusty?" Mark asked.

"Likely live!" Dusty got to his feet, holstered his guns and rubbed the trickle of blood from his cheek. "Splinter nicked me."

Sciffen looked up at the tall, powerful Texan who had crossed the room and now towered over him, "Don't hurt me again, Texas," he moaned. "Get me a doctor."

"Get one for yourself," Mark replied. "You aren't hurt bad. Allow your bar-dog needs a doctor more than you."

The Kid entered the saloon and walked to the bar. He looked over it with detached interest. Mark joined him, looked over at the smashed, torn arm and growled, "You danged Injun. Damned if I don't buy you a civilized gun!"

The Kid grinned; he was used to this reaction when he used his old Dragoon and a soft, round lead ball. "You do that."

The three Texans walked from the saloon together. From houses, stores and the other places where they had been hiding, men and women poured out to view the remains of Moxel's gang.

Sam Snenton and his wife came from the sidewalk before the Texas House. "Moxel's dead?" it was a statement not a question. "He was the man who gunned your wrangler, and Ben Holland. Moe, one of his gang, told us in there. He'd been drinking and talked more than he aimed to."

"Earp in on it?" Dusty asked.

"Not that I know of," Snenton replied. "They never said. I wouldn't spit in Earp's eye, if his face was on fire, but I don't figger him on a play like that. Way I see it was, Earp knew Ben was bad hurt and reckoned he'd never get back to Texas alive. That was why he put out the word. He reckoned to make a big play of it when Rocking H didn't come up this season. I don't reckon he'd got so far as hire Moxel to do the shooting."

"You've got more faith in him than we have," Dusty growled. "You might be right though."

"With Moxel and his bunch all down, there's no way to find out," Sam Snenton replied, feeling relieved that the trouble was over. "Earp pulled out of town yesterday at noon, and Moxel hasn't been in for a couple of days. Leave it lie, Dusty."

"Not quite!" Dusty looked round at the citizens of Dodge. "Where at's the Mayor? I've got things to say to him."

"Be up to the Long Branch, I reckon," Snenton answered and decided his judgment might have been out when he reckoned the trouble was over. "Do you want to see him?"

"We do!" Dusty sounded grim.

"I'll come with you." Snenton was one of the City Fathers and, while having an idea what Dusty wanted, didn't want to miss hearing it. He turned to his wife, "You looking peaked, honey. Feeling all right?"

"Yes." She watched one of the undertakers who was coming along the street. Her face was pale and she kept her eyes from the victim of the Kid's white stallion. "I don't want to go back inside until——"

"That's right, honey." Snenton's voice was gentle. "You stay out. Go shopping until after Hop Lee's cleaned the place up."

Mark pulled an old boot from his saddle pouch; it was small and dainty. "Could you take this to the Leathershop, Miz Selina? Tell Jenkins I want a pair of Texas-style, hand-carved boots making, stars and all, I want them ready for tonight."

Selina accepted the boot and looked at it, then at Mark's large expensive footwear. "They look a mite small for you."

"Not him, they useta call him ole fairy feet," the Kid scoffed.

"I'll see to it," Selina was pleased to have something other than killing and bloodshed to occupy her mind. "I don't know if Jenkins can do it in the time."

"You ask him to try, just for us," Mark drawled, a grin flickering on his lips. "Tell him, if they aren't ready, we'll have Kiowa and Billy Jack come sing to him."

The Mayor and other civic dignitaries were gathered at their table in the Long Branch saloon. They looked up with well-simulated pleasure as Sam Snenton and the rest of the Texans entered. The City Fathers were not over-eager for this meeting; all could guess there would be some trouble.

Dusty, Mark and the Kid halted in front of the table. For a time all was silent. Then Dusty spoke: "I'm trail boss for the Rocking H herd out there. The name is

Dusty Fog. Last night my wrangler came here and was
murdered. A year ago my kinsman, Ben Holland, was
gunned down in this town. The man who shot both of
them is still here. I've just killed him."

There was silence again. Dusty had thrown down the
gauntlet, but not one of the Dodge City men wanted to
take it up. "We're real sorry about what happened," the
Mayor said ingratiatingly. "And we should give you a
vote of thanks. Moxel had just about frayed his cinch
here. We——"

"I didn't finish." Dusty's drawl cut off the words
unsaid. "I hold this town responsible for what happened.
The man who was suspected of gunning Ben was left
to stay on here. Then, after he killed a man, you tell us
he'd frayed his cinch. Mister, you're going to see how
Texas men feel about it."

The men at the table looked at each other; not one
spoke for a long time. They had seen their police force
take it on the run from town and knew Dodge City was
in danger of being painted with the Stars and Bars, then
pulled apart, board by board, and scattered over the
range.

"Couldn't you hold your men in, Cap'n Fog?" one
man asked nervously.

"Why the hell should I?" Dusty's soft voice bit at the
men like a bullwhacker's whip. "You never played
square with Texas men here. You've taken their money
and, when they were broke, either had them jailed, or
run out of town. Now you're going to see riled-up Texans."

"But—but——!" the mayor spluttered.

"I'll tell you what I'll do. That boy who died yesterday, I want him buried in the real graveyard, not in boot
hill. I want him to have a real headstone. On it you'll
put *'Lil Jackie, the wrangler. He never lost a horse.'*
Will you do that?"

The mayor and council nodded their agreement.
Headstones were expensive items in Dodge, but not so
expensive as refusal would be. The City Fathers knew

that Dusty's word, once given, would never be broken.

"We'll do it, Dusty," Snenton promised.

"I'll talk to the boys," Dusty said. "Let's go."

The three young Texans walked out of the saloon, their bootheels thudding across the sidewalk. Then, with a creak of saddle leather, they rode out of Dodge.

Thora and Billy Jack rode at the point of the herd. They were on either side of the big red lead steer. Billy Jack pointed ahead to the sprawling town by the shining metals of the railroad. "There she be, Miz Thora," he said proudly. "There's been trail-end towns before, and there likely'll be trail-end towns again, but there ain't but one Dodge City."

Thora nodded soberly: she was still feeling the death of the young wrangler; it spoiled the drive for her, made her almost wish she had never brought the herd. "We should have sent more men," she said.

"Dusty wouldn't have wanted that," Billy Jack replied. "He's the trail boss and it was him that let Lil Jackie go in. We don't hold that against him, but that's how he thinks."

"Did he tell you that?"

"Didn't have to; I know how he thinks. Don't you worry, the skin hunter warn't never born who could lick Cap'n Fog."

Thora managed a smile; Billy Jack's face wasn't quite so miserable as usual. "I don't reckon there is. Say, I wonder where those old boots went."

"Did you lose a pair of boots?" Billy Jack asked innocently. "You should take better care of your gear."

Thora glanced at him, but she couldn't read the face. Billy Jack had taken the boots and given them to Mark with orders to get a pair of real Texas made-to-measures for the boss lady. "Look!" She pointed. "It's Dusty, Mark and Lon—they're all right!"

"Sure. Didn't you reckon they would be?"

CHAPTER SIXTEEN

A Trail Boss

The shipping pens at Dodge. A crowd was waiting to welcome the Rocking H, first drive of the season. The mayor and his council were assembled, and many other local citizens were there. All eyes were on the long line of cattle and the tall, tanned riders handling the herd with such easy familiarity. And on a tall, tanned, beautiful woman who rode as well as any of the men. For a moment there was silence. Then as Thora chased, caught, turned and returned a reluctant steer back to the herd the cheers rang out.

Thora's face flushed in a blush as she saw the familiar stubby shape of Doctor Burglin standing talking to an affluent-looking cattle buyer. She stopped blushing and smiled broadly when the fat, purple-dressed and much bejeweled madame of a downtown cat house yelled a delighted greeting to Billy Jack, while showing off some of her pretty assistants in a rig.

Dusty yelled: "Mark, Billy Jack, get ahead. Make a count."

Thora joined Dusty by the pens and watched the herd coming between the two counting men. The cattle buyers surged forward and the local people cheered. A speech of welcome from the mayor took her attention from the herd and she managed to say a few words of thanks for the greeting. Then she was having her hand shaken and requests made to buy her herd on all sides.

Mark and Billy Jack came up, thrusting through the crowd. They halted before Thora. "Boss," Mark said, "at a rough guess I'd say three thousand, two hundred and fifty."

"Don't make it no more'n three, two, forty-nine," Billy Jack objected. "I bet's you've been using the Big Bend count again."

"That's why I'm right. That Brazos count always ends up wrong."

"Brazos count?" Thora looked at each man, wondering if there was something here she hadn't learned.

"Why sure," Mark's solemn face should have warned her. "See, these Brazos hands, they count the horns and divide by two. Now us Big Bend men know that when you do that you miss the muleys."

Thora frowned, "I'm being took, but I'll bite. How do you do it?"

"We count the legs and divide by four."

"Which same works real well, unless you've got four steers with a leg short each," she put in thoughtfully.

"What difference would that make?" Mark had been so sure he had put one over on Thora, that he asked before he thought what she'd said.

"It would make you one short in the herd." Thora turned before Mark could recover. Dusty was standing behind her, smiling as he listened.

"Waal, Thora, that's your herd to Dodge."

"Why sure. We left Texas with three thousand, two hundred and thirteen. I'd tell a man you'd fed us beef all the way north. I reckon I'm sprouting horns. You lost a few and you've made Dodge with more than you left Texas with. Captain Fog, sir, you are a trail boss."